Watch for More Novels by R. M. Clark

From Indigo Sea Press

indigoseapress.com

To Emilia

The Right Hand Rule

By

R. M. Clark

Thanks for reading!

RM Clark

Skeeter Hawk Books
Published by Indigo Sea Press, LLC.
Winston-Salem

Skeeter Hawk Books
Indigo Sea Press
302 Ricks Drive
Winston-Salem, NC 27284

First Skeeter Hawk Books edition published
October, 2015

Rascal Books, Moon Sailer, and all production design are trademarks of Indigo Sea Press, used under license.
For information regarding bulk purchases of this book, digital purchase and special discounts, please contact the publisher at indigoseapress.com

Cover design by Pan Morelli
Manufactured in the United States of America
ISBN 978-1-63066-383-4

To every teacher I have ever had. You were all awesome in your own, unique ways.

—R. M. Clark

Acknowledgments

I would like to thank all the wonderful folks at Indigo Sea Press for their tireless work on this manuscript: publisher Mike Simpson, graphic designer Pan Morelli, editor Laura Tebow, formatter Teddy Hill and webmaster Scott Douglas. I also thank my beta readers: Sandra Clark, Danielle DeVor, Roland Lacroix and Kim Cogburn. You folks had the patience to sift through the drafts and help me point this story in the right direction. Bravo! Of course, I must give props to my e-friends, including the Purgies, the Ynots, and all the BBs at The Home for the Weary. Finally, to my family I say thanks for your constant love and support.

Chapter 1
Ziggy

Ziggy reached into his school backpack, pulled out a slightly wrinkled sheet of paper and flattened it out on the kitchen table. He figured it was time to read and fill out the contract.

I, Zachary Alfred Zygmont, understand that as part of the course requirements for Advanced or Gifted Science at John F. Kennedy Middle School, I am required to complete an individual experimentally-based research project. I understand that the project must be conducted during the current school term and described in a written paper...

The rest of it was pretty much *blah, blah, blah,* oral presentation, *blah, blah, blah,* no plagiarism, *blah, blah, blah.*

Okay, so far, so good, he thought. Ziggy signed it with his favorite black pen, over-emphasizing each first letter, especially the Zs. Science fair contract complete.

Yes, Ziggy's middle name is Alfred. So is his dad's and his grandfather's. That's three generations of Zygmonts who share a name with Batman's butler. Of course, the middle name never mattered because all three went by Ziggy. Except to his mom, he was rarely Zachary and never Z-Man and certainly never Alfred.

Just Ziggy. "May I sign it now?" his mom, Cynthia, asked while giving him "the look." No one ever called her Ziggy. Never. Just Cynthia.

Although he shared the same name as the other two Ziggys, he was the spitting image of his mother. Her hair was longer, of course; but they had the same eyes, nose and chin. The term "wiry" was a can't-miss description of all the Zygmonts; but Ziggy and his mom were taller than his dad, something with which Ziggy occasionally took joy in reminding the elder

1

Zygmont.

"Sure thing, Mom." Ziggy slid the science fair contract over to her, and she held it to the light to read it. He pretended not to notice how much she had to squint. Her glasses were probably on the computer desk or the washing machine or her dresser or in her pocketbook. Last Christmas he had bought her one of those glasses-holder-uppers like the librarians wear, but it never made it out of the box (and was quite possibly regifted). So she squints instead.

"Zachary, this was due weeks ago. Why am I just seeing it now?"

He could see her glasses on the counter behind her, next to a box of brownie mix, but decided it was to his advantage if she couldn't see clearly.

"A mere formality, Mom. I finished the project, kept a journal and wrote my oral report. Which, by the way, I presented to the class and Mr. Froth earlier today." He pounded one fist into his other hand. "Nailed it." He slid his favorite pen across the table to her, but she didn't pick it up.

"You didn't answer the question."

The thought of being busted made him shiver. "The truth is: I found it in the bottom of my backpack this morning after Mr. Froth reminded several of us that if we didn't get our forms in, we'd all get an 'F.' Once I turn it in, I'll get an 'A' because, as I mentioned, my science projects rocks." He slid the pen a little closer. "That's why."

She picked it up and signed her name below his, her smirk evident. "So when do I get to see this project of yours? You told me it had something to do with magnets, but that's all I know. Since then, you've been pretty secretive about it."

That part was true. Ziggy had given her some idea of what he was doing, but he preferred a captive audience for the presentation. "It'll be on display tomorrow night at the Science Fair open house."

"Your father and I will be there."

***

The next day was Thursday, and Ziggy had Mr. Froth's science class first period. He took his usual seat in the back left corner, farthest from the door. He seemed to do his best thinking there. Mr. Froth had been teaching seventh grade science at JFK Middle School for almost forty years. He was always getting asked when he was going to retire; but he would just shake his head, laugh his famous laugh and say, "Never!" in a serious voice. Ziggy and the other students believed him.

A true creature of habit (and a true member of "old school"), Mr. Froth began each class with roll call. He stood at his podium in front of the white board and read each student's name aloud, starting with Amy Aaron and ending with Ziggy. Amy took great pride in always being the first name called. For one semester in the sixth grade, Karen Aalas moved in to claim number one; but she left at February break, and Amy was back to top of the list. Ziggy was always last. No one could take that from him, unless someone named Zymon or Zyscovitch moved to town. Not likely.

"Kyle Christianson?" Mr. Froth read.

Kyle mumbled something and Mr. Froth continued.

Ziggy waited patiently for the other names to be called, and he always put that time to good use. He had calculated it took an average of 43.5 seconds to get from Amy to him. While others had barely unzipped their backpacks, he had managed to review the day's assignment or outline a chapter or perhaps get in a bit of flossing. Good oral hygiene was important in the Zygmont house.

"Greg Morgan?" Mr. Froth said.

"Here."

Ziggy had an odd way of categorizing people, based on where their names fell in the alphabet. The uplisters and midlisters came before him. He was a downlister and proud of it. He didn't envy the uplisters or midlisters. They couldn't help what family name they were given. Okay, that's not entirely true about the envy. When they announced the student awards at the assemblies, the applause was always much less for the downlisters than those at the top; but that's about it. Ziggy learned to live with it.

"Zachary Zygmont?"

"Here, Mr. Froth."

Forty-five seconds for roll call. That Mr. Froth, he was consistent. With roll call out of the way, it was time for the subject of science. The room darkened slightly, and Mr. Froth used a small remote in his right hand to lower the projection screen from above the white board. After a few clicks on his laptop, a Mayan temple filled the screen.

"As I've noted on several occasions, the Mayans were way ahead of their time," he said in a low, raspy voice. "They calculated the exact duration of a year to a thousandth of a decimal point." Mr. Froth then made one of his trademark moves. He stood in front of the screen, and the images flashed on his face as he spoke. It's hard to believe he wasn't permanently blinded by the light. "The Mayans did not, however, predict the world will end in 2012. That one is pure bunk." The steps of the pyramid were right on his forehead, leading up to the wisp of hair on top of his head. "They were, quite possibly, the most inquisitive culture in all of the Americas. They asked questions, found answers and never stopped learning. If you were ever lucky enough to encounter a group of Mayans, you'd certainly come away smarter. I can almost guarantee that."

He stepped aside and pressed a button on the remote. It was time for a segment he called "Mayan of the week." A Mayan wearing an elaborate head dress and colorful costume was on the screen. He did not look friendly.

"This is Kisin, the Mayan god of earthquakes and death. His name rhymes with 'reason,' but I doubt there was much of that in him. He rarely ventured anywhere without a spear and knife. Fortunately for you, this is strictly a visual exercise. Why do I say that? Ha! Because our Mayan of the week was known as the 'stinking one.' And that's just what his friends called him." The students all shared what Ziggy called a "Frothy" laugh. Mr. Froth continued. "He didn't contribute much to science, however. I just like the way he dresses. This is one guy you hope to never run into in a dark alley. Or a hallway. Or anywhere else, for that matter." Another click and he focused on the death collar Kisin was wearing, which had eyeballs hanging from it. *Nice touch*, thought Ziggy.

Mr. Froth had the unique ability to talk about the Mayans' contributions to science and not make it sound boring. He was also fascinated with Mayan culture and vocabulary. In fact, he started giving quizzes on Mayan words the first week of school. His lecture continued on for another thirty minutes as he carefully sprinkled in Mayan science tidbits. Ziggy had heard some of it before, but most he hadn't. Mr. Frederick Froth was bringing his A-game on this day.

His class lecture was always perfectly timed, leaving just enough room for a few short announcements.

"We have collected all of your science fair papers and displays," Mr. Froth said. "Thank you once again for your efforts. We'll announce the top four finishers tonight. Good luck to everyone."

The bell rang and first period was over. As Ziggy began to leave, one of Marshall Mason's gangly arms brushed him on the way out the door. For years Ziggy had been the tallest kid in class. Then Marshall shot by everyone in the summer before seventh grade. His shoes were as big as skateboards, and he was constantly running into things and people. Ziggy started calling him "Eminem" at the start of the year. But it never really caught on. That and Marshall threatened to smack Ziggy with his shoe if he didn't stop.

"Hey, Marshall," Ziggy said, taking a step back. "Ready for

the science fair?"

"You bet," he said in his deep, monotone voice. "But I probably won't win. I never do well at those kinds of things."

Typical midlister, Ziggy thought. *Always downplaying his contributions.* Ziggy slapped him playfully on the shoulder. "Your display is awesome, Marshall. I saw it when I dropped mine off. And don't forget: you aced the oral report, bro."

"Thanks, Ziggy. I gotta go." He nearly knocked over a desk on his way out. Being the biggest kid in school clearly had some disadvantages. "I'll see you tonight at the science fair."

Ziggy put his index and middle fingers together and gave Marshall his trademark two-finger salute as Marshall nearly stumbled into the hallway.

***

Ziggy's dad maneuvered their SUV into the teachers' parking lot, which was open to the public after school hours. As in years past, the science fair was set up in the cafeteria so the displays could be spread out over many tables, rather than cooped up in a classroom. The doors opened at six, so naturally they were twenty minutes early, even though Ziggy had informed them that no one was allowed in the cafeteria until the judges finished up.

"We get here early, and we get a good parking spot," his dad said with a final turn of the wheel. "Easy in. Easy out."

Of course, nothing was easy in the big SUV. Ziggy's mom called it "the beast." It was too big, too old and too much of a gas guzzler. His dad looked at Ziggy in the rearview mirror and winked. From that angle Ziggy could see a fresh batch of gray hair invading his temples, but he knew better than to mention it.

There were closer spots behind the school near the back entrance, but Ziggy didn't have the heart to tell him that either. They entered through the front door and quickly mingled with

6

the small crowd waiting in the lobby. The cafeteria doors remained closed.

Marshall spotted Ziggy from across the lobby and waved. Behind Marshall, a pair of big blue eyes caught Ziggy's attention. Amanda Yarrow smiled and waved. Ziggy's parents were chatting with another couple, so he broke free and made a beeline for Amanda. He heard "Hi, Ziggy" quite a few times as he walked along; but he just gave a general wave to all of them until he reached Amanda.

"Ziggy!" They gave each other a quick hug, the only kind allowed at their school. "Ready for this?"

Ziggy took a deep breath and slowly let it out. Seeing Amanda always made his heart race. "I think so. How about you?"

Amanda was one of Ziggy's downlist buddies, occupying the alphabetical spot in front of him for as long as he could remember. She just cocked her head, raised an eyebrow and smiled her perfect smile. No response was necessary because Amanda Yarrow was always ready for everything. Every test. Every quiz. Every report. Every project. He considered her a true downlister.

They chatted for a few more minutes before the doors to the cafeteria swung open. "I'll catch up to you later," he said to Amanda, complete with a two-finger salute. She flipped her hair and turned away.

The crowd had grown considerably larger from the time they got there, and it took Ziggy longer than he thought to wade through the masses to find his parents. They were nearly through the door when they met up.

"She's pretty hot," Dad said, leaning into him. Ziggy found it awkward when his dad tried to act cool.

His mom heard this and gave his dad an elbow to the ribs. "I don't like that kind of talk. Amanda's a very nice girl. Don't be rude."

"She is really nice, Dad," Ziggy said. "Smart too."

7

His mom went on ahead of them, well out of earshot. "She's nice and smart," Ziggy whispered, "*and* hot." He added a gentle elbow to his dad's ribs for effect.

The science fair projects filled up nearly every table in the cafeteria. They appeared to be scattered around randomly, so it took a while for Ziggy to find his. Like all the others, it was displayed on a tri-fold poster board.

"'Magnetic forces at work,'" his mom said, reading the large letters across the top. "Interesting topic, Zachary."

They stayed at Ziggy's display for a few more minutes, no doubt absorbing the interesting discussion on The Right Hand Rule and its use in everyday life. Ziggy found Marshall a few tables away, explaining his project to one of the parents. His was called **The Effects of Natural and Man-made Surroundings on GPS Receiver Readings**; and Marshall nearly knocked it over with his right arm as he made a point, but he caught the poster board just in time.

"Ziggy!"

Ziggy looked over one table and saw Amanda waving. He made his way to her table and saw her poster board for **Amanda's Amazing Memory Test**. She had given memory tests to adults and students to see who fared better. Ziggy had been one of her subjects a few weeks earlier, and so had Mr. Froth. Ziggy knew he fared pretty well. He examined her display and was not at all surprised to see that it was flawless, complete with text and graphs and artwork. He was sure she would be a finalist. Heck, he was pretty sure she would win the whole thing.

"After seeing this one," Ziggy said, "I'm tempted to toss mine in the dumpster. Nice work, Amanda."

"Thanks, Ziggy. And don't you dare toss yours. I really like it. The right hand rule made for a nice sidebar."

By sidebar she meant a tiny write-up on the side of the display. Ziggy even used his own right hand as a model for the drawing.

A teacher interrupted them and began to compliment

Amanda and her project. Ziggy took the opportunity to check out as many others as he could. He walked by Amy Aaron's project on astronomy titled **How to Locate the Center of a Galaxy Based on the Distribution of Globular Clusters.** *Wow!* thought Ziggy. *That is some title.* Amy stood quietly next to it and looked up at Ziggy through her oversized hipster glasses. Being one of the shortest girls in the class meant she pretty much looked up at everyone. Ziggy read over some of the complicated material, arched an eyebrow, then smiled at her.

"Nice job, Amy," he said.

"Thanks, Ziggy," she said. She nervously pulled her near-waistlength hair over one shoulder before flinging it back. "I'm so glad you like it."

She started to say something else, but someone pounded on a table near the front. It was Mr. Froth. The cafeteria got quiet as Ziggy found his parents and stood near them.

"Thank you all for coming to the science fair. We've had a chance to score each project based on three key items: written report, oral report and topic display. The top four students will advance to the regionals later this week. I'm told they are once again adding a fourth item, practical application, to the regional scoring. That part is always interesting." He stopped to add his trademark Froth-y grin. "Anyway, the students advancing to regionals are Amy Aaron..."

Everyone gave a polite round of applause.

"...Marshall Mason..."

More applause.

"...Amanda Yarrow..."

Wait a minute, Ziggy thought. *Three down, one to go. That could only mean one thing!*

"...and Zachary Zygmont."

Ziggy's dad slapped his back. "Congratulations."

"I'm so proud of you, Zachary," his mom said. Ziggy could tell she wanted to hug him but probably thought better of it with so many of his friends around. He hugged her instead.

"I'll need to see the top four finishers on Saturday morning," Mr. Froth announced. "Please be in the front lobby at 10 AM. The regionals are much more accelerated than in years past. I'll explain it all that morning. Until then, I thank you for participating. Remember, in the field of science, there are no losers, just those who don't progress as far."

***

The four who survived the cut at the science fair arrived at the school just before ten in the morning on Saturday. Amy, Marshall, Amanda and Ziggy met in the front lobby, just outside the principal's office. The heat must have been turned down, or maybe off, on weekends because Ziggy could see everyone's breath as they stomped around, trying to keep warm.

"This way, please." They all turned to see Frank Karalopolous, the school maintenance man in the hallway. He never wanted to be called Mr. Karalopolous or even Mr. K, so everyone called him Frank. "Mr. Froth wants to see you guys in the science lab." Frank was a big man with a big mustache, and his booming voice seemed to startle the students. "Don't just stand there; let's move it."

Frank clapped several times as he headed down the hall. They quietly followed him past the cafeteria to Mr. Froth's science lab. The light was on, so they all went in except for Frank, who closed the door and left. The room was eerily silent.

The science fair projects were displayed on the front table, and they all seemed instinctively drawn to their own as they stood in front of them.

"Where's Mr. Froth?" Amanda said. "And why is he is making this so weird?"

Before anyone could answer, the ceiling projector clicked on, and the image of Mr. Froth was displayed on the front screen.

"Hello, science fair finalists," he said. "Congratulations on your achievements so far. I'm recording this live from another part of the school, the location of which is not important at this time. What is important is that you realize the difficulty of the task ahead of you. As your science adviser, it is my duty to prepare each of you for the upcoming regional science fair. Your projects were chosen for their overall excellence, of course; but there is much more to it."

Ziggy managed to sneak a peek at the others; and they, like him, were completely mesmerized. He knew Mr. Froth was on the strange side with that tuft of white hair on the top of his head combed back and the huge knot of his tie pulled up tight to his neck, but the science teacher had certainly outdone himself this time.

"Science is too often a concept or an idea with no sense of the real world," Mr. Froth continued. "Practical application. That is the key this year." The camera zoomed out to show Mr. Froth standing in the center circle of the basketball court in the gymnasium. He walked around it, then went back to the center spot. "I was truthful the other night when I said the regionals started later in the week. What I didn't tell you is this." The camera zoomed in on his upper body. "The regionals start right now. Your task is to find me. Work together, use what you've learned and apply it." The camera zoomed out as Mr. Froth stood cross-armed on the center circle. "Good luck."

Mr. Froth snapped his fingers and disappeared.

Chapter 2
Marshall

Marshall shook his head and gave out a short laugh. "Amazing." He had seen Mr. Froth pull some interesting stunts before, but this one was the best.

Amy's right arm came up slowly, and she pointed at the blank screen. "Wha-, what was that?"

"You heard Mr. Froth," Marshall said. "It's a test. We have to find him."

"It's brilliant," Amanda said. "Absolutely brilliant." She turned and looked right at Ziggy. "Finally we have a teacher who's not afraid to challenge us. I'm *so* looking forward to the test."

"What?" Amy said. "I don't like the sound of this. I'm calling my mom right now." She pulled her phone out from the front pocket of her sweatshirt, but Ziggy put his hand over it before she could use it.

"You can't do that," he said. "The test has started. Besides, there's nothing to be afraid of."

"Yeah," Amanda said. "Remember what he told us: 'Use what you've learned.' We have to do this together."

"And I suggest we start in the gym," Ziggy said. "That's where Mr. Froth was last seen."

"Good idea," Marshall added.

Amy started to punch something into her phone, then stopped and put it back in her sweatshirt. "Fine."

The initial shock appeared to be wearing off as they made their way out the door and down the hall, Marshall leading the way.

"Why are we walking?" Amanda said. "Let's go."

She took off in a flash, and the others had to struggle to

catch up. *The hallway never seemed this long during school hours,* Marshall thought. *Now it went on forever.* They took a left at the Industrial Ed room and came to the double doors leading into the gym. Marshall went first and held one open for the rest of them. The gym was decorated in school colors, maroon and gold, and was empty except for a camera mounted on a tripod near the center of the basketball court.

"He's not here," Amy said, palms up and extended.

"Well, that wouldn't be much of a test, now would it?" Amanda said. "So, science fair finalists, what do we know?"

They walked as a group to the camera. The red light was still flashing on the front of it.

"He had an accomplice," Ziggy said.

"How can you be so sure?" Marshall asked.

"Easy. The camera was zooming in and out and following Mr. Froth as he walked around."

"I'll bet it was Frank," Amy added.

"Yeah? Well, how did he make Mr. Froth disappear?" Marshall said.

"How should I know?" Amy said. "I'm just throwing it out there."

"I think Amy's right," Ziggy said.

"Thanks, Ziggy."

She tossed her hair, and some of it brushed against Ziggy's arm. Marshall just rolled his eyes and looked away.

"Let's just check the video," Amanda said as she moved toward the camera. "It has a viewfinder." She flipped open the small screen and found a menu button to display the saved files. She selected the only one and hit Play. Marshall and the others huddled around to get a good view.

Mr. Froth was holding the camera at arm's length, pointing it back at his face. "Which is my good side?" he asked, moving his chin from right to left. "Ha! Neither!" Then he gave his trademark lame laugh. "But I do know my gee bass from my em sass from my rinex. Do you know the score?" Then the

13

screen went blank.

"Where'd the picture go?" Amy asked.

Amanda tried to get it back, but the menu was blank. "Self-deleted."

"It sounded like a whole lot of gibberish to me," Ziggy said. "Was that even English?"

With the camera no longer of any use, they spread out to think. Marshall stood near the center circle and went over what he had heard. That was not gibberish, and it most definitely was English. In fact, there was something familiar about those words.

"What did he say exactly?" Marshall asked.

Amanda paused for a moment and repeated the message, "I do know my gee bass from my em sass from my rinex."

"Those words don't make any sense," Amy said. She took her sweatshirt off and placed it on the first row of the bleachers. It was pretty warm in the gym so the others followed suit and tossed their sweatshirts and jackets next to it.

"Why would he start us off with such nonsense?" Amanda asked.

"Gee bass, em sass, rinex. Gee bass, em sass, rinex," Marshall repeated. He snapped his long fingers, and the sound filled the gym. "They're not words *per se*, you guys. They're acronyms. I used them all in my GPS project. G-B-A-S stands for Ground Based Augmentation System. M-S-A-S is Multi-functional Satellite Augmentation System and R-I-N-E-X means Receiver Independent Exchange Format."

"So our first clue involves using a GPS receiver," Amanda said. "Good thing we have Marshall around."

Marshall thought back to the message they watched on the viewfinder. "Mr. Froth said something else after the acronyms."

"Do you know the score?" Amy said. "Yeah. That's real helpful."

"What score?" Amanda asked.

14

Marshall repeated the question several times, then focused on the last two words: *the score, the score, the score.*

"The scoreboard," he said. They all turned around at once to see the scoreboard, which was above the bleachers, filled with numbers. The time read 44:11, which didn't make any sense. Marshall was all over it, writing something down on a small notepad. He was sure he alone knew what it meant.

"Latitude and longitude," he said. "GPS coordinates are given in pairs, one for east-west, latitude, and one for north-south, longitude. Each lat or long around here is made up of seven digits." He pointed to the scoreboard. "Can you see them?"

The score was 41 for the home team to 71 for the visitors. The "Player" box had 53 on the home side and 23 on the visitors. Each "Fouls" box displayed 1.

"Yeah, just a bunch of numbers," Amy said. "Whoever was the home team got their butts kicked."

"Seven numbers on each side," Amanda said. "Degrees, minutes and seconds."

Marshall had deciphered the coordinates and held out the paper for everyone to see. "These are the school's coordinates. I've seen them a million times."

"So Mr. Froth is still at the school," Amy said. "This won't be hard at all."

"Not necessarily," Ziggy said. "I seriously doubt we'll find Mr. Froth at those coordinates. More than likely, it's another clue."

"Practical application," Amanda said. "Mr. Froth emphasized it more than once." She moved her jacket off the first row of the bleacher seats and sat down. Marshall and Ziggy sat next her; then Amy reluctantly joined in. "Marshall," Amanda said, "do you have a GPS receiver on you?"

"No. But I have the ones I used for my project in my locker."

"Your locker?" Amy said as she jumped to her feet. "Are

you kidding me? You actually keep expensive electronics in your locker? Isn't that, you know, kind of risky?"

"Why, what's wrong with that? I needed a place to put them after the science fair. Besides, it's locked."

Amy hung her head. "I don't know about you guys, but I've heard that the superintendent, the principal and even the janitors all have master keys to the lockers. They come in after hours and comb through the lockers looking for anything they can get their hands on to sell on eBay and Craigslist. Nothing is safe."

Marshall's face went blank. He had never heard that tidbit before.

"That's an urban legend," Amanda said. "Students have certain rights, you know."

"I'm just saying," Amy added.

"Well, let's go check it out," Ziggy said. "Then we'll punch in the numbers and see where they take us." He flexed his fingers back, and the knuckle-cracking sound made Amy wince just a bit. They picked up their sweatshirts and jackets. "I don't know about you guys, but I'm dying to get out of this gym."

Marshall led the way toward his locker, which was all the way back near the principal's office. He slowed for a moment just after they made their way down the long corridor. He could see the large dent in the side of the end locker next to Mrs. Bailey's history classroom. In his first year at the school, Marshall was bullied frequently by a tough kid named Chase James. Marshall took it in stride, like so many middle school kids did, and tried to avoid Chase. The name-calling, taunting and shoving continued and got even worse as the months went on. When Marshall returned for seventh grade, he was much taller and stronger. He got some much-needed advice from an unlikely source: Mr. Frederick Froth. The science teacher had heard about Chase James and took Marshall aside on the second day of school.

"There are certain laws of physics that are absolute," Mr.

Froth told him. He took a ruler and balanced it on a pink eraser on his desk. "Objects at rest tend to stay at rest." He put a 9-volt battery on one end of the ruler. Then he took a large, D-size battery and slammed it down on the other side of the ruler, sending the smaller battery flying. "And objects in motion tend to stay in motion. That's today's lesson, Marshall."

Marshall knew exactly what he meant.

Chase James tried to bully him in the first week of school; but Marshall, the D-battery, pushed back, sending Chase, the 9-volt's body in motion across the hallway and into the side of the locker with a crash. Marshall got an in-school suspension for violating the school's no-contacts rule, but no one picked on him after that. Certainly not Chase James.

He lumbered ahead with his huge strides, a smile evident as he took another peek at the note with the coordinates written on it before tucking it back in his pocket. He realized it was his chance for "practical application," and he certainly didn't want to let the team down.

"Almost there," Marshall said as they turned into the main school corridor. The principal's office was in sight, and Marshall ran ahead to his locker just before it. He paused to think about the combination, then twisted the dial, opened the latch and swung open the big, red door with a clang. "Uh oh."

The only thing in his locker was a small notebook and two broken pencils.

Chapter 3
Marshall

Marshall reached into the void, moving his hands around the locker. "I put them on the top shelf. They were here in a white bag yesterday, I swear."

Amy said nothing, but she had one of those "I told you so" looks some girls were so good at making, complete with folded arms and tapping foot. Marshall was pretty sure this was part of the Froth plan and not an act of out-and-out theft—for eBay, Craigslist or otherwise. Still, he had to wonder.

"How many GPS units were there?" Ziggy asked.

"Three," Marshall said. He closed the locker, then opened it quickly, perhaps figuring they would just reappear. They didn't. "Each unit did the best, depending on the surroundings. One was good around rock formations, another near buildings and structures and the other in foliage like trees and stuff." He slammed the locker and pounded his head against it. "My mom is going to kill me."

"It's part of the test," Amanda said. "Everything that's happened so far has been planned out by Mr. Froth, so there's no reason to think this wasn't. Marshall, is anything else missing from the locker?"

"No. I put everything in my backpack yesterday." He opened the locker door and began to bang his head on the locker next to his. "My dad is going to kill me."

"They took everything except that one notebook," Ziggy said, pointing to the bottom of the locker.

"That's my doodle pad," Marshall said. "I haven't used it much lately. I've been a little busy."

Amy was closest and got the notebook first. She flipped through pencil sketches of werewolves, demons and assorted occult-looking figures. They were quality drawings, but Marshall seemed embarrassed that everyone was looking at them. After several blank pages, Amy flipped to the last page in the notebook. Instead of a Marshall drawing or doodle, there was a full color image of the gymnasium scoreboard.

Marshall grabbed the notebook. "Now how did he do that?"

"He's staying one step ahead of us," Amanda said. "Should we expect anything less from Mr. Froth?"

It was a rhetorical question, so Marshall and the others remained silent.

"So what does it mean?" Amy asked.

Everyone was in various states of deep thought as they pondered the latest clue. Marshall noticed that the numbers on the scoreboard image were the same ones he saw earlier. He started to say something, but Ziggy interrupted.

"Marshall, you told us these coordinates are for the school. But where exactly in the school are they located?"

Marshall slammed his locker shut. "Flagpole. The one in the quad. I used it as an example on the project."

The quad was the open area between the buildings. There were tables, benches and, of course, a flagpole, from which Old Glory flew every day.

"Well, what are we waiting for? Let's go," Amanda said as she pushed past the others.

The door just down the hall led out to the quad. A blast of cool air greeted the foursome as they made their way outside to the flagpole. Old Glory was flapping in the breeze, but slightly disrupted by something next to it.

"Look," Amy said, pointing up. "It's a pouch of some sort."

"That's my GPS bag," Marshall said. He untied a rope from the white cleat near the base of the pole. "How did they get up there?"

They all seemed to know Mr. Froth put them there or arranged to have them put there, so nobody answered. Marshall loosened the rope from the cleat, and the white bag came sliding down the pole. His large fingers fumbled to loosen the cord holding the bag closed. He wanted to swear but held it in due to "mixed company." With a final yank, the bag opened.

"All three GPS units are here. Safe and sound." He looked up and mouthed a quiet "thank you" as the breeze continued to whip the flag above them. The rope clanged into the pole with a rhythmic beat.

Amanda picked up the Balboa model and examined it. "This one's on."

Amy grabbed the Lancaster. "So is this one. And the arrow is pointing into the woods." She held it out in the same direction as the arrow. "Like a weather vane."

"Three for three," Ziggy said. That GPS unit was a Morton. "This one is pointing right behind us."

"Let me see." Marshall said with hand outstretched. He put it flat on a planter near the flagpole, then took the other two and lined them up next to it. He picked up the Morton and turned in the direction of the arrow on the display. "This one is closest. Two hundred thirty-seven feet in this direction." He set off in long, loping strides. He paused to look back as the girls gathered up the other two GPS units and fell into line. Ziggy brought up the rear.

"The display shows direction and distance," Marshall explained as they passed the gymnasium to their left. "It's a simple concept. You just follow the arrow until the distance is zero."

Marshall was clearly in his element as he took guidance from the hand-held device. The wind kicked up as they passed between the buildings, but it didn't seem to bother Marshall. He stopped with his back to the science building, then walked back the way they came. The others stood and watched as he turned in crazy circles for a few more seconds.

"It's jumping all over the place," Marshall explained. "I can't get a good read."

"What causes that?" Amy asked.

The Right Hand Rule

"The buildings mess it up." He pushed several buttons on the GPS unit while slowly shaking his head. "Wait a minute, you guys. Practical application." He smacked his right temple with the GPS device.

"What about it?" Ziggy said.

"My project is the solution."

"The effects of natural and man-made surroundings on GPS receiver readings," Amanda said, recalling his project title.

"That's right. The Balboa out-performed the other two under these conditions. Tricky, tricky Mr. Froth. He mixed them up for me." He took the Balboa from Amanda and began to enter the coordinates until the arrow reappeared. He looked up and pointed down the corridor. "Twenty feet this way."

It took them to a spot just outside the last window in the science building. The high walls of the gymnasium were but fifteen feet away. Marshall moved to his right, then returned to the spot. The winds picked up between the buildings, so Marshall zipped his jacket up to his neck.

"This is as close as the Balboa will get us," he said. "Something has to be here."

"What are we looking for?" Amanda asked.

"Something out of the ordinary," Marshall said.

"That's not very helpful," Amy added.

Marshall thought about answering but just repeated what she said in a mocking tone. Fortunately no one heard him. Amy could be so annoying.

They began to look around, checking the ground and behind the small bushes that lined the building.

Amy was the first to notice something unusual. She pointed to the classroom. "Guys, look at the windows. All the shades are down and curtains drawn except for this one. I think our answer may be *inside* the room."

The lower part of the window was uncovered, and there was only room for three heads. Marshall got there first, cupped his hands around his eyes and peered into the science lab. It

21

was dark, but he could make out the science fair projects right where they had left them earlier. Nothing seemed out of place.

Amy and Amanda found a section of window and peered in. "The word of the day," Amanda said. "It was blank when we were in there this morning. Now there are two words." Mr. Froth always had a "word of the day" on his chalkboard. It was usually relevant to the day's lesson and vocabulary test. Other times it was a Mayan word he thought was cool.

"*Chumuk* and *chumúuk*," Amy said. Then she spelled them out.

"Those are Mayan," Ziggy said. "I recognize them from vocab."

"What do they mean?" Amy asked.

"I'm pretty sure the first one is center," Amanda said, "and the other must be something similar."

"Middle," Marshall said.

They pulled away and stood near Marshall as he looked at his GPS unit. His mind raced and his lips moved slightly, like he was talking to himself. Then he thrust his right arm straight up.

"I know what it means," he said as he gave a trace of a smile. "More practical application." He started punching buttons on the GPS unit while nodding along. "Good one, Mr. Froth. Tricky, tricky, tricky."

"Um, Marshall," Amy said. "Care to enlighten your fellow scientists?"

"My project, Amy. One of the tests I talked about in the oral report was finding the circumcenter of a triangle using waypoints from GPS devices. That's the center or middle he's referring to. It was pretty much theoretical on my project. But now..."

"Practical application," Ziggy said. "He's making you do it for real."

Marshall punched a few buttons on the GPS unit, then gave it a smack. "Come on!"

"You *do* know how to do this, right, Marshall?"

He held the GPS unit out at arm's length. "Of course."

Chapter 4
Marshall

After a few silent minutes, Marshall collected the other two GPS units and placed them flat in his palm. "See where they're pointing? To the other ends of the triangle. We have to finish the triangle and find the center."

"How can we help you?" Ziggy asked.

"Someone has to stay here with this device." He held out the Balboa to see who would take it. He secretly hoped Amy would.

"I'll stay," she said. "Just don't leave me here all day, okay? Please." She smiled her crooked little smile at Ziggy, who smiled back. Then she flipped her hair over her shoulder. Marshall took Ziggy by the shoulder and turned him. This was no time to be flirting.

He gave Ziggy one of the hand-held units and led the way past the buildings to the front of the school. He took them across the street and onto a bike path heading directly away from the parking lot. He stopped here and there to check the display but kept walking in the same general direction.

Marshall's fascination with GPS devices began the previous summer when he took up the hobby of geocaching, where you use a GPS device to find containers hidden at specific coordinates everywhere in the world. He had tried to explain it to Ziggy and Amanda once, but they seemed disinterested. Marshall had found hundreds in the surrounding area, and he got hooked on it big time. He occasionally wore a shirt that read:

**I use billion dollar satellites to find
Tupperware in the woods
What's your hobby?**

23

"This has to be taking us to Patton Rock," Marshall said. "I should've known."

Patton Rock was a large granite rock formation a block or so from the school. It was in a patch of woods that belonged to the town. Oddly enough, there were no other big rocks anywhere near it. You walk along the trail through the woods and suddenly it's there. Marshall had heard it was named after one of the town founders, but everyone passed on the story that it was shaped like General George Patton's helmet. The thought of that tidbit made Marshall grin.

"Why would Mr. Froth choose Patton Rock?" Amanda asked.

"One of the tests was how well each GPS unit did around large rock formations. This is the biggest one around here by far." The rock was about twenty feet high with a gentle slope on both sides (like a helmet, remember?) so it was easy to climb. Marshall stopped just before it and pointed to the display. "Tricky, tricky Mr. Froth."

"Now what?" Ziggy asked.

"He put the Patton Rock coordinates in the worst performing unit under these conditions. Just like he did for the other one. Tricky, tricky."

Ziggy started to hand Marshall the Lancaster device, then pulled it back. "I saw how you did it," he said. "I can enter the coordinates."

"It's not as easy as you think."

"Piece of cake." Ziggy used his thumbs and put in the coordinates to match the other unit. When Ziggy handed it back, Marshall's face lit up; and he pointed to the path along the right side of Patton Rock.

"This way." Marshall's long arm remained outstretched as they followed him up the path.

They reached the edge of Patton Rock, and Marshall's eyes looked toward the top. "Up we go." He started to climb, so Ziggy helped Amanda up the first stage, then followed.

Marshall walked in a circle before settling at a spot near the center of the rock. There were beer cans and broken bottles nearby, remnants of past parties. A few scrub bushes and a tree grew out of the large crack that ran along the top of the rock. "Here. This is the spot," Marshall said. "He even marked it." There was a faint FF written with chalk. "Two sides down and one to go."

"I'll stay," Ziggy said. "You two go and get the next one."

Marshall let out his first laugh of the day. "That won't be necessary."

"Why not? We need to find the circumcenter, right?"

He held up the Lancaster. "The GPS devices hold all the information. Once we find ground zero, we're good to go."

"So why is Amy still back at the first point?" Amanda asked.

Marshall smirked and said nothing as he headed back down the rock. Ziggy caught up and grabbed him by the shoulder. "You were just trying to get rid of her, weren't you?"

Marshall smirked again and practically ran down the rest of the way. They caught up with him before he could get away. "What can I say? She just...bugs me," he said. "Besides, she *thinks* she's helping. That's all that matters."

Amanda did her best to keep from laughing. She summoned a serious face and stepped in front of Marshall. "We're a team, remember? You can't just leave someone out because you feel like it. This first test is yours, and I'm betting we'll all get our turn. Please don't do that again, okay?"

He stared into his GPS device for a good five seconds.

"Marshall!" Ziggy said, clapping his hands loudly.

"Okay, okay." Marshall still had a silly grin, and he had to admit to himself that his plan was brilliantly cool. Or cool-ly brilliant. Either way, Marshall proved he could be tricky, tricky like Mr. Froth. "We're a team. Got it."

Their next stop was to rescue Amy from her duties as GPS place holder. Ziggy held Amanda back as they got closer to see how Marshall handled it.

"Took you long enough," Amy said, stomping her feet to keep warm. "I'm freezing, here."

"Sorry," Marshall said. "Mr. Froth switched the units again, so it took us a little longer." He took the Balboa from her. "We're off to find the third one now. I have everything I need in here, so you don't have to hang anymore."

"Thank God for that. I was tired of doing all the work." She bent over, and her back cracked loudly.

Marshall had a hard time holding back a major laugh; but he walked away, then made believe he was tying his shoe. He looked up and saw Ziggy and Amanda also on the verge, but all three managed to grin and bear it as they began the trek toward point number three in the woods behind the school. Marshall had all three units under control, with two in the front pockets of his cargo pants and the other in hand. He was busy with the Lancaster, the unit Ziggy programmed with the Patton Rock coordinates. Ziggy nearly bumped into him when Marshall stopped at the beginning of the trail.

"Ziggy!"

"What, Marshall?"

"You didn't save them. I can't believe you didn't save them."

"Save what?"

"The coordinates to the third point. You put in the numbers for Patton Rock, but you didn't store the other ones as a waypoint. I told you it's not as easy as you think." His thumbs moved quickly, but his head shook slowly. "It's no use, the final point is gone. Poof!"

"I'm sorry, Marshall, I just—"

Marshall put his huge hand near Ziggy's face to cut him off. "Don't try to Ziggy your way out of it. It won't work on me." He went back to his GPS unit. This was followed by more head shaking and swearing under his breath.

"You can get them back, right, Marshall?" Amy asked as

26

she moved in next to him. "Tell me you can fix this."

"Gone, gone, gone," Marshall said. He smacked the device against his knee.

"I don't believe this," Amy said. "Why did you let him do it, Marshall?"

"Wait," Ziggy said. "All is not lost. Give me a minute and it'll come to me."

"You heard him," Amy said. "Gone!"

Ziggy made a steeple with his fingers as he thought. Then he snapped his fingers. "Forty-one," he said. "That's what the first coordinate starts with. The second starts with seventy-one. If we think about it, I'll bet we can come up with the rest of the numbers. Or at least get close."

"Close isn't good enough, Ziggy," Marshall snapped. "One misplaced digit and we're looking hundreds of feet in the wrong direction."

"I was afraid something like this might happen," Amy said.

"Everyone stop!" Amanda stood between the others with her arms out in front. "We're a team, remember? I've been thinking. The three points of this triangle are very close together, so from what I know about latitude and longitude it's only the last two digits that will be different, right, Marshall?"

He looked at the display. "I suppose that's true." He fiddled with the device briefly. "Maybe this won't be so bad."

"We're science fair winners," Ziggy said. "We can do this."

Marshall turned his back on Ziggy and spoke only to Amanda and Amy. "He's right." Marshall thumbed in Ziggy's direction. "The first digits are forty-one and seventy-one. The whole town starts with those."

"And the middle two digits," Amanda said, "are fifty-three and twenty-three respectively, right?"

Marshall looked at the display. "Right. The minutes."

"Now I remember," Amy said. "The other two were forty-four and eleven."

Amy had her arms crossed like she was absolutely positive.

Marshall checked the displays of all three GPS units.

"Sorry, Amy," said Marshall. "Those are for the flagpole. I still have them entered in here." He held the device out, but no one looked too closely. Amy just turned away uninterested.

"The numbers were only on the Lancaster display," Amanda said. "We all saw it at least once. You need to use associative memory techniques to recall the numbers."

"How do I do that?" Marshall asked.

"Simple. Think about where you were when you saw the numbers. This would have been after we found the first point of the triangle near the science classroom."

Marshall thought back to when they were looking in the window. Right after that, they started out for the Patton Rock. He saw the numbers on the display. *What were they?* There was a three on one side and a one on the other, but he couldn't piece it all together. "Thirty-seven and nineteen." It was a complete guess.

"Are you positive?" Amy asked as she stomped her feet to warm them up.

"Um, no. Not positive."

"Then don't guess. God, Marshall, we'll be here all day."

Part of Marshall wished they would have left her at the first point, holding the Balboa and flipping her stupid hair until her feet froze off. But then again, she was on the team, so she probably had some skill (besides being annoying) that would be useful. Eventually. What was Mr. Froth thinking?

"Think about the display," Amanda said. "Picture the arrow pointing to the location. Associative memory relies on remembering big details to bring out the smaller ones. What color is the display? How many sections is it divided into? The numbers are there. What are they?"

Marshall went so far as to close his eyes to try and remember. He followed Amanda's instructions and pictured the display. It was a light background with dark gray numbers and letters. It was divided into three sections, with the arrow at the bottom and latitude and longitude at the top. He could see the numbers now. They were so close.

"Seventeen," Marshall said. "And the other is eleven. Now I remember."

"Are you sure?" Amanda asked.

"Yes." Marshall punched in his coordinates, then looked dejected. The arrow pointed in the wrong direction.

"Right numbers," Ziggy said. "Wrong order. It's eleven for the lat and seventeen for the long." He clapped his hands one time. "Try it, Marshall."

Marshall used his thumbs to put in the new numbers, and the arrow pointed where he thought it should go. "This is it, I'm pretty sure. Lucky recovery, Ziggy."

"Well, sorry for the screw up," Ziggy said. "Looks like we're good to go." He put out his fist and Marshall hesitated, then bumped it. Fist bumps were so sixth grade.

They walked north into the woods where the Lancaster excelled at finding the right spot without bouncing all around. Amy was watching the display with Ziggy as they led the way. Amanda and Marshall lagged behind. She had a smirk that let him know something was up.

"You knew the numbers all along, didn't you?" he asked in a low voice so the others couldn't hear.

"What makes you say that?"

"Because I showed you the display as we walked to Patton Rock. Well-played."

Her silence and her grin confirmed his suspicion. She was making them work as a team, in spite of themselves. They joined the other two, and Marshall explained the workings of the GPS as they made their way down the trail. He even made it sound interesting, like he was channeling his inner Mr. Froth.

"This is the spot," Marshall said as they arrived at a clearing just off the trail. It was thick with tall pines and scrub.

"What are we looking for?" Amy asked. She wasn't at Patton Rock so this was all new to her.

"A marker of some kind," Marshall said. "With Mr. Froth it could be anything."

"That's not much help."

He wanted to say, "Neither are you, munchkin," but he kept looking, instead. There was a blue arrow painted on the side of a tree, but it was just a trail marker. A bit of sunlight poked through the clouds and brightened up the clearing. Marshall turned to his right and saw a white, plastic band around one of the branches of a medium-sized pine tree.

"Found it," Marshall said.

Amy came over and examined the white band. "That's it? How on earth did you ever see it? All I see are trees, trees and more trees."

Marshall shrugged his large shoulders. "You just get used to it." He held out the white band for the others to see. It had the initials FF for Frederick Froth. This was, indeed, the spot.

"Okay," said Marshall, "all three waypoints have been confirmed. Now all I need to do is find the circumcenter."

"You figured how to do that, right, Marshall?" Amanda asked.

"Yeah, I was working on it on the way here. Thought I had it figured out, then realized I was using the wrong device. The Morton has a built-in triangulation algorithm, not the Balboa. Duh." He tapped the unit against his head a few times. "Sometimes I can be so dense."

"So where is the circumcenter?" Ziggy asked.

Marshall's thumbs went crazy for a few seconds. "It looks like a spot near the playground." He handed Ziggy the display. The compass arrow was pointing just a bit left of straight ahead. The distance was 0.12 miles, or just over 600 feet.

"Anyone up for a jog?" Ziggy asked, not waiting for an answer. He tore ahead of the others but not too fast, as if he wanted them to catch up.

It wasn't long before Amy blew past hm. She was the fastest girl in the school and was being recruited for the high school track team next year. Amanda was next, followed by Marshall, who ran maybe fifty feet, then walked the rest. The others watched and rested as he made his way down a brick sidewalk next to the playground.

"It's one of these engraved bricks," Marshall said. The walkway was made up of red rectangular bricks, some of which had names engraved on them. It was part of a fundraiser for the playground a few years ago. For fifty bucks you could buy a brick and get what you wanted written on it. Most of them were engraved with names. The others followed Marshall along the red brick path, moving right, then back to the middle. "This is the circumcenter. Plus or minus a few feet."

"How will we know?" Amanda asked. "There are so many bricks."

"I think Mr. Froth would find a way to make it stand out," Marshall said as he checked each brick in the vicinity.

"Look," said Amy. "This one is outlined in chalk."

"'To the class of 2016 by Ms. Doreen Daniels,'" Marshall read.

"Who's that?" Ziggy asked.

"She's the lunch lady. I'm pretty sure she's been around forever. I mean, my mom remembers her."

"Wow, that is a long time."

Well, Marshall's mom wasn't *that* old, but he knew what Ziggy meant. Ms. Daniels was always there in the cafeteria to greet everyone with a cheerful "Hello" and a smile as she dished out bad pizza, boring hamburgers and questionable meatloaf. Marshall couldn't think of anyone who didn't like her. The science fair finalists gathered around the brick and tried to figure out its significance. It looked like most of the others.

"She has other bricks too," Amanda said from a few feet away. "This one is for the class of 2015. Here's another for 2014. Looks like every class gets one."

"Maybe the '2016' means something," Ziggy said. "They could be clues to new coordinates."

"I think we're done with coordinates," Marshall said. "We found the circumcenter."

Ziggy reached down and swept some dirt off the brick. "So what does it mean?"

"Besides being our graduation year," Amanda said, "I don't know."

"Guys," Marshall said. He was pointing back to the school. The big window on the side of the cafeteria was still visible. Someone was standing in it, waving.

"I'm pretty sure it means lunch time," he said.

Chapter 5
Amanda

Amanda put her hand up to shield the sun as she looked back at the school. The person in the window gave them a "come here" wave, then disappeared. *It was perfect timing,* she thought. All four of them were striving for the same goal and all seemingly arrived at the same non-scientific conclusion: it was lunch and they were hungry.

"Look at the time," she said. "Eleven-fifty. The second lunch bell would be going off right about now."

She wasn't sure if Mr. Froth planned that or if it were a giant coincidence. Neither would have surprised her. After a morning of searching for the midpoint of Marshall's GPS-generated triangle, it would have been a welcome relief. After lagging behind a bit, Amanda ran to catch up with the others.

There was no one in the cafeteria when they arrived a few minutes later. This didn't surprise her either because she knew Mr. Froth was too clever for that. They just wanted food. There were four brown paper bags on a table in the center of the room. None of them were marked. They each grabbed a bag. Marshall reached into the first one.

"Sandwiches," he said. "This one's chicken salad. Blecch." He slid the bag away.

"Chicken salad's my favorite," Amy said. "Anyone want this turkey?"

Amanda took a turkey sandwich nearly every day so her decision was easy. Ziggy chose ham and cheese, and Marshall jumped all over the peanut butter and jelly.

"Somehow he seemed to know what each of us likes," Amy commented a few minutes later. She didn't add anything , and the others just nodded. It was eerie but so like Mr. Froth.

"I need to call my parents," Amanda said with her phone out. "This was supposed to be a morning thing. Now it looks like an all-day thing. You know how parents get."

Everyone took the opportunity to make a call or two. After they finished, they found some drinks and snacks and got down to the business of lunch. After a very trying morning, it was good to just chill out and get a little bit goofy. Ziggy did a few impressions of some teachers. His best one was Mr. Froth talking about the Mayan god of war.

"Our Mayan of the week, Kisin, is known as the 'stinking one,'" Ziggy said in a perfect Froth voice. "And that's just what his friends called him."

They all had a nice laugh as they finished up lunch. Amanda balled up her paper bag and lofted it toward the nearest barrel. It bounced off one side, then went in. "Two points."

Ziggy rewarded her with a high-five, then launched his own trash ball, landing it cleanly in the middle of the barrel. Amy and Marshall made theirs too.

"Is anybody else wondering what's next?" Amy asked randomly.

Amanda was having so much fun the question caught her off-guard. "I guess I am too. But I'll bet Mr. Froth has devised something clever."

Almost on cue they all began to look around the cafeteria for the next sign from their science teacher. Amanda found it, literally, on the bulletin board. "There," she said. "The large poster board wasn't there yesterday. Most of the notices are pretty tiny."

They went over as a group to check out the large, white poster. There was a single word written in small print in the center:

pa'achi

"Another Mayan word, I presume," Amy said.

"I don't remember this one," Marshall said.

Ziggy pronounced it out loud a few times. "I do. It was an extra credit word on one of his vocab tests. It looks familiar. I think it means joke."

"No," Amanda said. "Joke is *p'a'as. Pa'achi* means below. No, wait." She snapped her finger at the revelation. "It means behind."

"Behind what?" Amy asked.

They turned in unison for the "big event," but nothing unusual was behind them. Marshall laughed, grabbed the poster and turned it around. "Behind this."

Written on the back were the words:

AS YOU LIKE IT 2/7

"Anyone know what this means?" Ziggy asked.

Marshall just rolled his shoulders.

"Shakespeare," Amanda said. "It means 'As You Like It', scene two, act seven."

"How do you know that?" Amy asked. "We don't take Shakespeare until our freshman year."

"My mom's an English teacher, remember? I've been reading Shakespeare's plays since I was ten. I even had a conversation with Mr. Froth about Shakespeare a few weeks ago. I can't believe he remembered."

"So what is so special about 'As You Like It,' act two, scene seven?" Ziggy asked.

"Does the line 'All the world's a stage' sound familiar?" Amanda asked. "It's in that scene and just happens to be one of his most famous quotes."

"The stage," Amy said. "Maybe he wants us to go there."

Amanda thought about the latest clue. It *seemed* logical. Mr. Froth's previous clues were fairly straightforward, so it was likely this one would be too. He was definitely challenging them, and she loved the thought of it. Too many teachers in her school were compelled to "teach to the test," meaning they were mostly concerned with how the students fared in state-monitored exams. Not Mr. Froth, apparently.

"I agree," she said. "Let's go."

Marshall nearly knocked over the poster board as he put it down on the table, and they filed out of the cafeteria to await their next adventure. Amanda couldn't help but notice that everyone was smiling.

***

Like a lot of middle schools in the area, John F. Kennedy Middle School was formerly the town's high school for many years. It had a tiny old gymnasium, a tiny old cafeteria and fittingly, a tiny old auditorium. Amanda couldn't remember it ever being used for a play, mostly just for talent shows at the end of the year. In fact, the stage doubled as a section of the library, with the rows of books along the back shelf covered during performances.

There were no permanent seats in the auditorium any more, just folding chairs that were brought in as needed. When Amanda and the other science fair winners entered, they saw four chairs in the center, facing the stage.

"I think we'll sit here," Marshall said.

Order didn't seem to matter, but they did manage to arrange themselves alphabetically. *Probably not a coincidence*, Amanda thought. The stage was dark and the old, red curtain was closed up tight. It gave off a musty odor that did not mix well with the smell of hundreds of books. Such was life in an old school.

It seemed like they were at a movie so Amanda brought up the obvious. "I don't know about you guys, but I could use some popcorn."

"Yeah," said Marshall, "with butter. Oh, and a large root beer."

"Gummi bears," Amy added. "Or Nerds."

"Definitely Jujubes," Ziggy said, completing the menu. They were all content with their imaginary favorites, but Amanda had a feeling this was not going to be a typical matinee. The lights dimmed and the curtain parted, squeaking loudly as it strained to open. A spotlight shone on the back wall, revealing a single word:

yaanal

Then the spotlight went off.

"Another Mayan word," Marshall said. "I wish I would have paid more attention in class."

"It means beneath," Amanda said.

Ziggy jumped in. "Or under."

"Under what?" Amy asked. "There are a thousand things in here."

"Under the chairs, more than likely?" Marshall said as he felt around the floor under his metal chair.

Amanda reached under the seat of her chair and pulled out an envelope. "Way under," she said with a smile. "It's attached to the bottom."

The rest of them pulled out their envelopes. Amanda opened hers and took out a single sheet of paper. "'Time to go to the sensory store,'" she read as the lights came up slightly.

The other three envelopes had the exact same message.

"What's the sensory store?" Marshall asked. Amy and Ziggy also gave her confused looks.

Amanda stood and faced the others. "It looks like it's time for Amanda's Amazing Memory Test. In my report I wrote about how memory works. You see, psychologists divide memory into three stores: sensory store, short-term store, and long-term store. When we remember something, some of it goes into short-term memory, also called short-term store. You know, like what you had for breakfast this morning or what numbers were on Marshall's GPS device. Anyway, from there, some of that information goes into long-term memory so we

37

can remember it next week, next year or decades from now when we're old like Mr. Froth." She didn't really think Mr. Froth was *that* old, but it made her point.

"So, Amanda," Amy said as they waited for something else to happen. "About your amazing memory test. What exactly should we expect? I'm sorry, I didn't get a chance to read your presentation."

"No problem. I focused on the science of human memory. I wanted to show how people remember things and who's more likely to have higher memory skills under certain conditions."

"What kind of conditions?"

"Well, I gave the same number test to both students and faculty. It was a series of ten random numbers displayed one second apart. Each person just wrote down the sequence at the end of the ten seconds. Both students and faculty scored about the same, which was one of my hypotheses. Then I proved that people will remember more numbers if given the numbers in 'chunks.' We remember phone numbers by grouping the numbers into a pattern of 3-3-4. Have you ever noticed how hard it is to remember a phone number if you get it in an odd sequence? Like if I say my number is seven...seven four five...five five three...six one nine, the sequence is out of whack and you would have a harder time remembering the number."

"I never thought of it that way," Amy said.

Before she could explain any more, a single spotlight shone on the stage to the right. On the edge of the stage was a stack of four laptop computers. Marshall got up and retrieved them.

Amanda's laptop squeaked as she lifted the cover. Surprisingly, there was an application open and a small, blank window in the middle of the screen. She looked at the other screens, and everyone had the same thing. Then the lights dimmed and the curtain groaned as it opened. Some text appeared on the stage wall:

Repeat each number sequence displayed
You have five seconds to provide an answer

38

"Looks like the memory test is about to start," Amanda said.

To her right she could see Ziggy's knee bouncing, making the computer shake in his lap. To her left, Marshall's right foot tapped a quick, rhythmic beat. And further down, Amy had a look of complete terror. Amanda took a deep breath and wiggled her fingers above the keyboard to loosen them. This was her time.

Chapter 6
Amanda

The numbers started coming at a fast and furious pace. Three-digit numbers flashed up on the big screen, and they had to repeat them in the window on the laptop. Then they moved on to four- and five-digit strings of numbers. Not surprisingly, Amanda flew through the early tests without missing any. The machines gave out a low buzz for a wrong answer; and she could hear several buzzes, especially from Marshall's machine. There were plenty of buzzes from the others when they moved on to the seven-digit numbers. Then ten-digit strings proved to be everyone's undoing as a chorus of wrong answer tones rang out, even from Amanda's machine. She knew from her project that memorizing ten-digit numbers in rapid fire format was nearly impossible. Apparently Mr. Froth knew it too.

When she first explored the idea of doing a memory test, Amanda went to Mr. Froth for advice. He was intrigued by her general hypothesis: younger test takers would perform better than older test takers in the number sequence test under normal conditions.

"Life rarely gives us normal conditions," he told her. "You should research abnormal conditions and how they affect memory. Music, temperature and even stress can affect the memory store. I know first-hand that a person's true colors come out when the going gets rough."

The thought of it made Amanda smile.

The lights came up a bit, and round one appeared to be over. Amy closed her laptop. "Is there a point to this? I mean, how is this going to help us find Mr. Froth?"

"These are baseline tests," Amanda said. "They set the standard for all the other part of the test."

"Which is?" Amy asked.

"Performance under duress." Her voice tailed off as she said it.

"Duress?" Ziggy said. "You mean like with someone chasing after us or maybe hanging from the ceiling? That kind of duress?"

"Of course not." Amanda gave him a gentle tap on the shoulder. "Think of duress as less than ideal conditions."

The memory test Amanda had given the students and teachers a few weeks earlier was a standard memorization test with no duress, unless you count the crazy air-conditioning in Mrs. Moore's room. Everyone was freezing that afternoon.

Some music started playing. It was soft at first, then slowly got louder. The instructions once again appeared on the back wall:

Repeat each number sequence displayed
You have five seconds to provide an answer

The windows in their laptops cleared, and the first set of number appeared on the stage screen. A very loud hip-hip song filled the room, providing what Amanda thought was a perfect level of duress. The music stayed at a constant volume, and a deep voice began to count down.

"Five…four…three…two…one."

No one was bouncing this round. She could hear the failure buzzes coming from everyone's machines as they progressed along through several rounds. Amanda had never experienced a test under such conditions, and the combination of the music and countdown voice caused her to miss a few out of pure panic.

Amy was the first to snap. "This music is driving me crazy. Can someone make it stop?"

Amanda knew the answer to that one. "It's just part of the test," she said.

"I know that. I'm just thinking out loud. I'll bet you were

thinking it too, Amanda."

"I don't mind the music," Marshall added. "But I wish that stupid Mr. Countdown would go away."

Amanda could feel Amy's eyes upon her and peeked to make sure.

"So aren't you going to tell him it's just part of the test?" Amy said. "You had no trouble reminding me."

Amanda knew Amy was never one to work well under pressure, or duress, in this case; but this was ridiculous. They had been in the same "smart classes" all through middle school, and Amy was always a nervous wreck on test days. Rather than responding to Amy's comments, Amanda just turned away.

"Chill out, Amy," Marshall said. "A new test is starting."

The next task was all about visual identification. They had to stare at an object or drawing, then another would appear a few seconds later with subtle differences. They had to find at least one of the differences. Most were pretty easy. There was a city scene with an added building in the "after" shot. A pretty kitten had blue eyes in one and brown in the other. They all did fairly well with a minimum of wrong tones.

"This one's a bit different," Amanda said, pointing to the screen. It was a blueprint of a building. "I certainly never used it in my tests."

After a few seconds, she recognized that it was a blueprint of the school. It stayed on the screen for about ten seconds. She prepared herself for the next slide, which she expected to be like the previous one, but with a few slight differences.

They waited and waited. Finally the slide changed, but it wasn't another blueprint. Two words appeared on the screen:
HELP ME

"Help me?" Amanda repeated. "That doesn't seem like part of the test."

"What the heck does it mean?" Marshall asked.

Before anyone could answer, a rumbling sound filled the

auditorium. It wasn't coming from the speakers. It was real. The entire room shook.

"What's going on?" Amanda asked. "Was that an earthquake?"

Amy listened closely, then began to shake her head slowly. "This isn't right."

"What isn't right?"

A smaller rumble—an aftershock, perhaps—knocked several books off the shelves. A magazine rack fell over with a thud. Amy said, "He needs our help; I can feel it."

"Who needs our help?" Ziggy asked. "Mr. Froth?"

"Amy, what's going on?" Amanda said. "You don't look so good."

Amy's face was ashen, and her lips looked bone dry. "We have to go back to the lab. I'll explain when we get there." She took a few steps toward the door. "Come on!"

They followed Amy down the main hall toward the science section, then turned the corner and sprinted toward Mr. Froth's science lab. The hallway lights were off, so it was easy to see the ultra-bright light coming from his lab. The ceiling projector was on, displaying an empty page onto the white display screen.

"I gotta hand it to Mr. Froth," Ziggy said. "He really outdid himself this time. The 'Help Me' message, the rumbling sound, the blank display screen. It's all so...convincing."

"Yeah," said Marshall. "I'm totally buying it." He put out his fist and Ziggy bumped it. He extended a fist in Amanda's direction but was met with stone silence.

"I don't think this is part of the test, you guys," Amanda said. "Something's not right here."

Amy stepped in front of the pack. "That's what I've been trying to say. None of this is planned. Mr. Froth needs us and he needs us now."

The conversation was interrupted by a noise coming from the supply closet in the back of the classroom. Amy turned to see Frank, the maintenance man, emerging from it. His hair was messed up more than usual, and the Red Sox cap he always wore was twisted to one side.

"Frank, what happened?" Amy asked.

Frank shook his massive head, probably more to get rid of cobwebs than to answer the question. He sat down in the nearest desk. "I tried to help, but they couldn't be stopped."

"Who couldn't be stopped, Frank?"

He removed the cap and wiped his brow with his hairy forearm. "Mr. Froth resisted, of course." He took a deep breath. "But they got him."

"Frank," Amy said in a serious tone. "Was he kidnapped? Who took Mr. Froth?"

Frank started to talk, then nearly choked. His arm came up slowly and pointed to the front of the classroom as he made stuttering noises.

They turned to see an image on the projection screen. Two men were standing on top of an ancient Mayan pyramid.

"It's Mr. Froth," Amy said. "But who's that with him?"

Amanda took a few steps toward the screen to get a better look. Someone dressed in an ancient wardrobe was pointing a spear at Mr. Froth's neck. The headgear looked familiar from some drawings she had seen. There was another rumble, only louder than the previous one. Then it clicked.

"That's Kisin," she said. "The Mayan god of earthquakes…and death."

Chapter 7
Amy

Amy and the others looked on as Mr. Froth was apparently being held prisoner at the hands of perhaps the most evil Mayan who had ever lived. A million questions flashed through her mind, like: How did he get there? And, well, that was the big one and none of the others mattered. Amy could read Mr. Froth's lips as the spear pressed against the collar of his shirt. *Help me.* Then the screen went blank.

Marshall was the first to panic. "Okay, what is going on here? This is all part of the test, right? Tell me this is part of the test." He moved too quickly and knocked over a desk.

"It's totally *not* part of the test," Amy said. "The test is over, and Mr. Froth needs our help for real."

Amanda spoke up after a long silence, "You seem to know a lot about what's going on, Amy. Care to fill us in?"

She looked over at Frank, who nodded weakly.

"Okay, okay," Amy said. "Frank and I have been in touch with Mr. Froth the entire morning. It's all part of the test. I've been texting him when you guys haven't been looking. He needs accomplices to pull this part off. He needs people he can trust to keep a secret. Am I right, Frank?"

Frank was a bit more composed now. "It's true. Whenever you guys are in one place, I give him the sign and he continues the test. Just so you know, we've been doing these science fair finals for a few years. I gotta admit, this is the strangest one I've ever seen."

"So much for keeping a secret," Amanda said in Amy's general direction.

"Did you even hear what I said?" Amy shot back. "The test is over. He needs our help. I'm pretty sure that trumps everything."

"How do we know this isn't part of the test? Your act has been pretty convincing, so far."

"Yeah," said Ziggy. "You've been in a few plays at the high school, I recall. A good actress could pull this off."

"It's not an act!" Amy got as close to Ziggy and Amanda as she could. "I told you everything I know, and you still don't believe me." Ziggy was right; she had been in several high school plays over the years, always typecast as a young girl due to her small stature. But this was no act, and she tried to stare down Amanda to make her point.

Amanda just stared back. "I'm still not convinced. In fact, I don't think—"

Boom!

The conversation was interrupted by the sound of Marshall smacking his size 14 shoe on the desk. "Stop it, you guys. None of this is helping." Amy was going to reply, but Marshall held his shoe up and looked at her as if he would slam it down again if she spoke. "I just want to say that this is not what I signed up for. I'm tempted to get up and just walk right out this door; but Mr. Froth is my favorite teacher, and I owe it to him to finish up."

"I hear you, Marshall," Ziggy said. "He's my fav—"

He slammed his shoe down three more times. It was nearly as loud as the rumblings they heard earlier. "I'm not done, yet! You know what I think? I think it's just another example of Mr. Froth being tricky, tricky. He made himself disappear on camera, didn't he? Why can't he put himself on a Mayan pyramid? Or the Himalayas? Or the Sahara Desert for that matter? Any first-year film student could pull it off."

"Marshall—" Amy tried to get a word in.

"I'm still not done." He slammed his shoe one more time. Not only was the sound annoying, the stink was starting to fill the room. "The gig is up, Amy. Game over." He stood and quickly put his shoe back on, then stood on the desk chair. "Come out, come out, wherever you are, Mr. Froth." His hands

46

were cupped to his mouth for maximum effect.

"Marshall!" Amy got up and pulled him off the chair. She was much stronger than she looked. "This is not a joke or a trick. This is real." Marshall put his hands on his head and pulled on his medium-length hair. "It's real? So Mr. Froth really disappeared? Twice, actually. Once in the gym and once in this classroom. Absolutely amazing. Like that magician guy, David Copperhead."

Amy had known Marshall since first grade, and this is the most she ever heard him say at one time, even if he meant David Copper*field.* "I told you what happened," Amy said. "The first was a trick to get us interested. This one, the pyramid thing and the Mayan god of death? Yeah, that was not part of the plan. No way."

Almost on cue, the projector fired up again. "Look," Amanda said. This time Mr. Froth was surrounded by a large crowd of Mayans. Well, they appeared to be Mayans because they looked just like the ones Mr. Froth showed them every week. Oddly enough, they weren't threatening him anymore. They started checking him out. One of them had his iPad and was showing the others. Mr. Froth frequently said they were inquisitive people.

"I can't bear to watch this," Frank said. "I'm going to call the police." He took out his cell phone and began to punch in numbers.

"I don't think that's a good idea," Ziggy said. "They would never believe it, anyway. 'Middle school science teacher is being held hostage by Mayan warriors.' I'm pretty sure they would just laugh at you."

"Then what are we going to do?" Frank pocketed his phone.

"Exactly what he bought us here to do," Ziggy said. "Find him and bring him back."

"The test is over," Amy said, coming between Ziggy and

Frank. "Can't you guys see that?"

"I don't believe that," Amanda said.

"I don't either," Ziggy said. "This *has* to be part of the test. Marshall, do you believe it now?"

He looked down at his now-intact shoes. "I suppose."

"The computer," Amanda said." I think we should start there and see if it can tell us anything."

They huddled around the desk while Amanda worked the mouse and keyboard. She clicked on a small icon at the bottom of the screen, and a still shot of Mr. Froth and Kisin jumped onto the screen. *It sure looks real*, Amy thought.

"How did he do it, Amy?" Amanda asked. "How did he project the images into the theater from here?"

Amy stood behind the others, with arms crossed and right foot tapping quickly. She had arrived before the others that morning and was given a set of instructions by Mr. Froth to make sure everyone was following along. He had chosen her for the task because of the complexity of her science fair project. In fact, it was Mr. Froth who convinced her to tackle the difficult subject matter of astronomy, and particularly globular cluster. He showed her how to present it in a clear and concise manner without pandering to the typical seventh grader. No one had ever challenged her like Mr. Froth. So when he asked her to arrive a few minutes before the others, she agreed. Her main task was to keep everyone interested in the test until they reached the auditorium for Amanda's test. After that she was on her own. Of course, everything was going according to plan. Until now.

"It's a simple network connection," Amy said." Other than that, I'm not sure. I was there with you, remember?"

Frank joined the huddle, coming in from the side. "Once you four were in the theater, he stood right there and watched. The questions were already loaded into the slide show. The only tricky part was the music, you see. I had to feed that in from behind the stage. Mr. Froth had a program that took care of the countdown voice."

"When did you notice something was wrong?" Ziggy asked.

"I was in the hallway, coming back from the theater. That's when I heard the first rumble."

Amy recalled the sound, and it sent chills down her back. Again.

"Anyway," Frank continued. "I ran here as fast as I could, and that fella right there in the crazy costume had a hold of Mr. Froth." Frank was pointing to the image of Kisin on the screen. "Mr. Froth, well, he put up a good tussle. I went to help him, but that last boom sent me headlong into the supply closet. I may have broken a Bunsen burner or two, but that's neither here nor there."

"What I want to know," Marshall said without any help from his shoe, "is how that Mayan guy got from there to here." He jabbed at the screen, then back to the ground.

"I think I found something," Amanda said from her seat at the desk. "There's an application called TimeScope open and running. Anyone ever hear of it?"

The students all shook their heads. Amy looked over at Frank, who just threw his hands up.

"I also found the slide show that played all the memory questions. It's stuck on the last slide he showed us, the one with the school blueprint." She clicked on it, and the blueprint shined on the screen behind them. It was plain with no music or countdown to put them under duress.

"Open up TimeScope," Ziggy suggested. "What's the worst that can happen?"

"What could happen?" Amy shot back. "Oh, I don't know, maybe a few more Mayan warriors. Maybe that's not such a good idea."

Amanda disregarded Amy's objection and opened the application. A Mayan pyramid appeared on the screen. It looked to be the same one where they saw Mr. Froth a few minutes earlier. This was no ordinary still photo, though. Amy noticed the image moved like they were watching through someone's eyes. They floated above for a few seconds, then returned to the ground, which was teeming with Mayan natives.

"It looks like a portal of some kind," Amanda said as she watched in fascination. "A window into the past."

"I've seen that before," Frank said. Amy jumped at the sound of his voice. "When we went over everything before you folks got here this morning. Mr. Froth showed me the memory test so I could synch up the music to it later. He used a small remote to make the slides change. He kind of clicked on the TimeScope thing by accident. It's funny, though."

After a pause, Amy asked, "What's funny, Frank?"

"Mr. Froth, he likes to stand in front of the screen even when we're just practicing. I don't know how it doesn't blind him."

"He does that in class too," Marshall said. "All the time."

Frank stood in front of the projector to demonstrate. The Mayan village shone off his high forehead.

"You know, Frank," Amy said. "That's probably not a good idea."

"What could happen?" he said with a laugh.

Amy reached out for his arm and attempted to pull him away. "No, really. Don't-"

And just like that, Frank was gone.

Chapter 8
Ziggy

"Frank?" Amy yelled. "Oh my god, you guys, he's gone too."

Amanda said, "I don't believe this."

"This can't be happening!" Marshall added.

Ziggy stood by, not sure what he had just witnessed. One voice in his head was telling him to just run out of the school as fast as he could and get help. Another voice, this one much calmer, was sure Mr. Froth would never do anything to hurt them. Or Frank. Or himself. The calmer voice won the battle.

"Just calm down, you guys," Ziggy said. He stood close to where Frank last stood and observed the situation. *It had to be some sort of trick*, he thought. *People don't just vanish.* "Mr. Froth disappeared in the gym a little while ago. Frank's in on the whole thing, so I'm thinking it's a trick. Just part of the test."

"I don't know, Ziggy," Marshall said. "I think we should call the police or something."

"And the FBI," Amy added

"No," Amanda said. "At least not yet."

Ziggy observed Amanda carefully. She made a fist and put it to her mouth. It was her trademark thinking pose. "What is it, Amanda?" he asked. "It looks like you're on to something."

"It's the projector," Amanda said. "We've been focusing on the computer, but it's the projector that's causing the leap; I'm sure of it."

The leap? Ziggy wasn't surprised she already had a name for whatever was happening.

"Who cares what's causing it?" Amy said. "All the grownups have disappeared. Doesn't that bother you people?"

You people? As much as Ziggy liked to think of them as team, they clearly weren't. *What people were we?* he wondered. Before he could respond, the room shook and the display changed. Mr. Froth and Frank were both surrounded by Mayans.

"That Kisin dude," Marshall said, while pointing a shaky finger at the screen. "He's got Frank too. This is bad, you guys. Really, really bad." He took his phone out, but Amanda stopped him.

"We have to rescue them," Amanda said. "Come on, everyone. We're honor science students. We have to use our skills."

"And what do you suggest we do, Amanda?" Amy said. "Follow them to Mayan country?"

"What we should do," Amanda said, "is exactly what Mr. Froth taught us. We all had to follow the scientific method for our science projects. Problem, hypothesis and solution. Okay, we identify the problem: two people from our school have been sent back to a Mayan civilization through some sort of time portal. Check. Next we form a hypothesis." She stopped and faced the rest of us. "So does anyone have one?"

This brought a major eye roll from Amy, but Ziggy swooped in to help. "Mr. Froth has been teaching the science of the Mayans for several weeks now, right?" The girls nodded, and Marshall made a grunting sound. "Well," Ziggy continued, "what if his TimeScope program really did allow him—and us—direct access to their civilization? Mr. Froth thought it was, you know, a one way connection and we could see but not be seen. The inquisitive but evil god Kisin doesn't like being spied on so he finds a way to enter the portal and check it out. As for Mr. Froth and Frank, well, that was just bad luck."

Amanda gave Ziggy a tiny clap and a smile. Even Marshall seemed to be buying into the explanation. One look at Amy assured Ziggy he was only getting two out of three.

"I don't know, Ziggy," Amy said. "I mean, really? Mayans

and time portals?"

"What's your hypothesis then?" he asked.

"Why does everything have to be so scientific?"

"So you don't have one," Ziggy said. He loved that he was getting the upper hand.

"I don't think I need one, Ziggy. Don't you guys get it? The science experiment is *over,* and two people are missing. This is serious stuff."

Ziggy's answer never made it out of his mouth. Marshall's sneaker was once again pounding away. Three loud smacks on Mr. Froth's desk put a quick end to the discussion. "Blueprint," he said in a very calm voice.

"Blueprint?" Amanda repeated.

"Yes. The last memory test he gave us was to identify the difference between two blueprints of the school. I think it's important."

Amanda started clicking on items on the desktop. "Marshall's onto something. The test should be on here somewhere." Files opened and closed with great speed. Finally the slide show they had seen earlier popped up on the screen. "So let's find out." She clicked through the slides until she came to the visual difference test. The school blueprint now filled the screen. "Before." She hit the next screen. "After."

The display was small on the computer screen, making it difficult to spot the difference. Amanda went back and forth between the two. "Right there," Amanda said, pointing to the upper right corner.

"I see it," Ziggy said. "There's a wall missing in the 'after' slide. That's over near the cafeteria. I don't think it's a classroom."

"That's the utility room," Marshall added. "Frank's domain."

"Now we're getting somewhere," Amanda said. "There must be a reason he chose that room. I say we check it out. Who's with me?"

"We can't leave now," Amy said. "What if they need our help?"

"We're trying to help," Amanda said. "Mr. Froth left some clues, and we need to check them out. If you want to stay here, fine. The rest of us are going."

Well, so much for volunteering, Ziggy thought. Amanda stood, followed by Marshall. Ziggy was right behind them. Amy sat with her arms folded tightly, not budging.

"C'mon, Amy," Ziggy said. "We're a team, so let's do this together. We need you."

"The test is over. I already explained it."

Ziggy had never seen Amy so stubborn. "The old one is over," he said. "The new one begins now."

Marshall cast a giant shadow over her. "He's right. We need you, Amy."

After some awkward silence, she finally stood. "Fine," she said as she pulled the sleeves of her shirt down and brushed them. "I guess it couldn't hurt to have a look."

They moved quickly into the hallway and ran as a group toward the cafeteria. Amanda stopped for a moment to get her bearings, then took a left down a short corridor where Ziggy had rarely ventured. There were no windows in this part of the school, so it was dark and a bit spooky. The door at the end was painted the same maroon color as the walls. Thankfully it had a shiny doorknob.

"This is the place," Amanda said. "One of Frank's hangouts." She twisted the knob and pulled open the door with a squeak. It was dark and Ziggy hit the light switch near the door. A gigantic furnace took up most of the room, with pipes running everywhere. The lights didn't do much to help them see, but there was something bright on the other side of the room. They moved around the furnace and toward the light like a swarm of moths.

A projector like the one in Mr. Froth's room sat on a table in the middle of the room and lit up a large screen on the far wall. The words "HELP ME" were in large red letters.

"What is this?" Amy asked.

"I'm not sure," Ziggy said. There was a partially-eaten lunch on a small table in the corner. Someone had been there recently. There was a computer on a small desk near the wall and "HELP ME" displayed on that screen as well. The screen saver hadn't kicked in yet, if it had one.

"Frank never mentioned this room," Amanda said as she checked out the computer. "Does anyone else find that strange?"

"Yeah," said Marshall, "he was pretty open about everything else."

"Or he was just telling us what we needed to know," added Amy.

Something caught Ziggy's eye as he gazed around the room. The projector was plugged into a power strip which, in turn, was plugged into a nearby socket. A yellow cable ran from the back of the projector to the corner of the room and up into the pipes running along the ceiling. "A network cable," Ziggy said. "I bet this leads either to the auditorium or Mr. Froth's room."

"Yeah, that makes sense," said Amanda. "No network connection in here. They had to hard-wire it."

"What are we waiting for?" Amy said. She was up and out the door. They followed at a fast pace until they got to the auditorium. Ziggy was not at all surprised to see that the chairs were still lined up in the front, and the screen displayed "HELP ME" in large letters, just like in Frank's room. He checked the wall on the left and saw the yellow cable coming out of the corner of the ceiling along with several others. It worked its way along the back wall and into the small "projector room" in the back.

"So they controlled the action from Frank's lair," Amanda said.

"But what about Mr. Froth's lab?" Marshall asked.

"Shouldn't that hook into here too?"

"All the classrooms are connected to the local network," Ziggy said. "He just has to plug into the wall."

"I don't think all this network talk is helpful," Amy said. "We need to help Mr. Froth before the rest of us go *poof!*"

Her *poof!* was well-timed. A loud rumble, like the ones from earlier, tore through the school.

"Sounds like it's coming from Mr. Froth's room!" Amanda yelled. They sped out of the auditorium and down the hall to his lab. Marshall was the first to arrive.

"I... I don't believe it," he said, his voice choking up.

The room was back in its normal state. There was no projector, no computer and no overturned desks.

"What is going on?" Amanda said.

Amy pounded the door hard with the bottom of her fist. "I don't know about you guys, but I don't like this test anymore."

For the first time that day, Ziggy had to agree with her.

56

Chapter 9
Amy

Amy was on the verge of tears after seeing the state of the room. She had a simple arrangement to supply information to Mr. Froth earlier in the test and nothing more. This was not what she expected. She didn't want to cry in front of the others and managed to hold back the waterworks after a taking a couple of deep breaths.

"Who could have done this?" Amanda asked as the others spread out in the classroom.

"Well, obviously someone's helping Mr. Froth," Amy said.

"Don't you mean someone *else*?" Ziggy said. This got him a stern gaze from Amy.

"Or maybe," Marshall said, "he never really left."

"But we all saw him on the screen," Amy said. She pointed to the blank screen, and it didn't really help make her point.

"Tricky, tricky Mr. Froth," Marshall said for about the hundredth time that day.

Then the screen slowly worked its way back up. Three words were written on the board behind it:

xibalba be 2012

"Anyone know what it means?" Marshall asked.

Amanda began to say the words out loud, apparently hoping for inspiration.

"It's Mayan, but a weird combination. Fear something?" Amanda said.

"Place of fear and 2012," Ziggy said. "I'm not sure what it means to us, though."

Amy said the words, then began backing away from the board. Her face was suddenly pale, and her hands trembled.

"No. No. No," she said softly. "I can't believe he did this. I... I just can't believe it."

"Who?" Ziggy asked. "Mr. Froth?"

"Did what?" Amanda asked.

"It's still on," Amy said. She finally stopped a safe distance from the screen. "The stupid test is still on." She composed herself and sat in the closest seat. The others also sat. "'Place of fear' is what the Mayans called the Dark Rift. I made a reference to it in my project. It was a teeny, little drawing in the lower corner"—she put her fingers a few inches apart—"but somehow Mr. Froth decided it was important to test me on it." With a sigh, her head flopped down, dangerously close to the desktop. "Marshall and Amanda had their turns, so now I guess it's mine."

She tried to think about what Mr. Froth could possibly test her on. The subject was so dark that practical application seemed almost impossible.

"I've heard of the Dark Rift," Marshall said, this time without using his shoe to make his point. "It has something to do with the Milky Way, right? And Earth's alignment."

Amy's head popped up, and she gave a half-hearted nod. "It has *everything* to do with the Milky Way. It's a complex subject; that's why I only touched on it for the report."

"Can you give us the quick and dirty version?" Ziggy asked.

"Quick and dirty" was a term Mr. Froth used frequently, Amy noted. She was not surprised Ziggy borrowed it.

"Okay, I'll try. The rift is that dark scar that runs through the center of the Milky Way. It's really a bunch of dust and gas clouds that block light. In December, 2012, the sun is supposed to align itself in the center of the Dark Rift for the first time in over twenty-five thousand years. The famous Mayan calendar ends at that time. Coincidence? Maybe."

"But didn't Mr. Froth say that was a bunch of bunk?" Marshall asked.

"It's a project on astronomy," Amy said, "and the Dark Rift is an absolute fact. The Mayan part is still, well, open for debate."

"What I want to know," Amanda said, "is how he plans on testing you on this. His being held against his will by the Mayans and the Mayan death god and all."

In all the excitement Amy had momentarily forgotten about Mr. Froth's capture. Or alleged capture. Did it really happen? Then there was Frank, the great disappearing man. Everyone seemed to have forgotten all about him.

"Let's not forget," Amy reminded them, "that Frank went *poof* right before our eyes. Seeing is believing, right?"

"I don't know how he did it," Amanda answered. "But somebody came and cleaned up this room while we were gone. Somebody knows our every move. I agree with Amy. This is all part of the test."

Marshall was unusually quiet, which meant he was either thinking or getting ready to pound his shoe on the table again. Once again, the size 14s remained grounded.

"I'm not so sure," he said as his right hand nervously explored his left sleeve and shoulder.

"About what?" Ziggy asked.

"About Mr. Froth and Frank." Now it was left hand and right sleeve and shoulder.

"Why do you say that?" Amanda asked.

Marshall freed his hands, then clenched them on top of the desk, rapping it with his knuckles. "I know it sounds weird, but I think they are both still gone. I mean, how do we know he didn't write that on the board hours ago? The screen has a motor to draw it back up after a certain amount of time. Remember when it went up by itself during the first mid-term exam? Freaked everyone out, didn't it?"

"That's right," Amanda said. "Mr. Froth said it wasn't worth getting fixed."

"I heard he had a remote for it and kept it in his pocket,"

Ziggy said. "He used it on special occasions."

"Maybe," Amy said. "But it doesn't explain why the computer is gone and the room was put back to normal. I mean, really. Who else could have done it?"

"The other custodian," Marshall said. "I've been here on Saturdays before, and there are always at least two custodians around. Maybe the other one saw the room was unused and straightened it up. It makes sense to me."

Ziggy walked over to Mr. Froth's desk and pulled his chair away. "Okay, let's go with that theory. If you were cleaning up, saw a computer out and wanted to put it away, where would you put it?" He pulled open the top drawer, and it was locked. He pulled open the next one, and there was Mr. Froth's laptop. "Right here!" He took it out and put it back on his desk.

"Open it," Marshall said.

He slid the lock to the right and lifted the lid. The ceiling projector roared to life and filled the whiteboard with bright light. The screen seemed to know what was going on as it worked its way back down.

Amy was the first to notice what was on the screen. "Oh my God!"

Mr. Froth and Frank were sitting on the top step of a pyramid, surrounded by several Mayan warriors. Amy was pretty sure they were warriors because they all had heavy face paint and wore colorful costumes. Two Mayans examined a smart phone in a bright orange case, the same one Frank pulled out earlier.

"Look," Amanda said, "Frank's trying to say something."

It was hard to tell with all the people milling about in front of him, but they all seemed to notice it at the same time.

"Help me," they said together.

Marshall began pounding his fists on the desk. "It's all my fault. I thought it was a good idea to find the other room, and all we did was put them in more danger. Amanda was right. We needed to follow the scientific methods Mr. Froth taught us to figure this out." He took a shoe off and began to smack himself in the head with it. "How could I have been so stupid?"

Ziggy grabbed Marshall's arm before he could deliver a second blow to his noggin. Based on his foot size, that could have been fatal.

"It's not your fault, Marshall," Amanda said. "We're a team, remember?"

"It's actually a good thing you did that," Amy said. "Or we would have never seen the words on the whiteboard and thought about the Dark Rift."

Marshall looked up. "So how does that help?"

Amy got up quickly and went to the empty whiteboard on the side of the classroom. She picked up a red marker and put a single dot in the center of the board. "It helps because I think I know how to get them back."

Chapter 10
Amy

Amy stood next to her dot and thought about what she was going to say next. Unlike some of the typical science fair projects, she had spent two full months researching and writing her project. It was a complex subject that needed to be simplified. Mr. Froth helped her greatly with that part.

"Let me explain." She began to draw and didn't stop until she nearly covered the entire whiteboard with her "explanation." She faced the group like she was going to speak, then went back and filled in a few details. "This is the Milky Way," she said, taking Mr. Froth's pointer and making a circular motion on the board. It had the pinwheel shape of the Milky Way and a thin band running through the center. "This is the Dark Rift. In December, 2012, the sun and the earth will move into direct alignment with the equator of the Milky Way galaxy. This phenomenon won't occur again for another twenty-six thousand years." She drew a line through the red dot (the sun) and the center of the Dark Rift. She tried to draw the solar system in the middle of the rift, but the dots became very small and she stopped.

"Interesting," Amanda said. "But what does this have to do with Mr. Froth and Frank and the Mayans?"

Amy, proud that she knew something Amanda didn't, ran the pointer down the line that bisected the Milky Way. "Alignment, Amanda. It all comes down to alignment. Or should I say, near perfect alignment. You were talking before about the scientific method; you know, stating the problem, hypothesis and solution, right? Well, the problem is obvious." She turned her pointer in the direction of the screen where Mr. Froth and Frank remained surrounded. "I wasn't ready to make a hypothesis before, but I am now. Here goes." She even cleared her throat for effect. "Just as the alignment of the sun in the center of the Dark Rift is supposed to cause some unfortunate phenomenon, I hypothesize that this town—more specifically, this school—is in alignment with the Mayan village we see on the screen. I'm not exactly sure how; but I'm positive we have to act now before the opportunity goes away, which brings us to the solution."

Amy finally decided to take a breath. The others sat quietly, apparently mulling over what she had presented. Marshall's shoes remained firmly planted on his feet. Amanda was unusually quiet about the discussion. Ziggy tried to keep from fidgeting.

Amy continued, "Think of it this way: 'something' here in the school has aligned." She used finger quotation marks to make her point. "This alignment resulted in a rift which is causing all the commotion here at the school. We need to find the source."

"That's it?" Amanda asked. "You make it sound so easy. How could we possibly know—"

"Blueprint!" Marshall said.

Even Amy was thrown off by his interruption. The last time he brought it up, they ended up running to the other end of the school. Now Marshall was pointing to the screen, finger wagging to a slow beat.

"The blueprint of the school," he said. "Can someone put it on the screen?"

Amy was closest to the computer, so she had the honor of digging through the desktop files for the slide they had brought up earlier in the day. A few clicks later, the blueprint of the school was on the screen. She had no idea what he was up to but went along with it.

Marshall stared at the blueprint with his chin in his hand. "Circumcenter. Most definitely the circumcenter." He took one of the GPS devices and began to punch in the buttons. Amy, previously unstoppable at the whiteboard, could only watch silently. Marshall gave a few grunts and finally an "Aha!" Amy always found him to be a guy of few words, but he was never more annoying than at that moment.

"Marshall," Amy said. "Care to share with us what you're doing?"

"You can't be getting a satellite signal this far inside the building," Ziggy added.

"Don't need one," Marshall said, without looking up from the display. "Look at the blueprint." He stood up and made his way to the whiteboard. He put out his hand, and Amy gave him the pointer as she moved to the side while flashing an "I don't know" look to the others. "Three points. Number one is the science lab. Number two is this room, and number three is that weird room in the back where Frank hangs out." He tapped each location on the screen as he said them, and the screen shook from the force of the pointer. Then he carefully circled a spot in the middle. "This is the circumcenter. Major alignment, right here in our school." He tapped the center point once more for effect. "Major."

"The auditorium," Amy said. It was all right there on the blueprint.

"Perhaps it's a coincidence," Amanda said. "I mean, it's an old, traditionally-built building; and the auditorium just happens to be in the middle."

"It's no coincidence," Amy said. "And thanks, Marshall, for noticing that. It really explains a lot."

"Not to me," Ziggy said. His hands formed a perfect T, with his right palm touching his left fingers three times. "Time out. Full stop!" He held the T for a good five seconds. "What does what *you're* saying"—he broke the T and directed his right hand at Marshall—"have to do with what *you* were saying?" With a slight rotation, his right hand moved to Amy.

"Alignment," Amy said.

"Circumcenter," Marshall added. They high-fived each other.

"Yes, I know," Ziggy said. "But you have to be a little more specific. I have two questions. One: What is aligning with what; and, two, what is in the circumcenter? Please don't make me take my shoe off and bang it on the desk. Thank you."

Amy and Marshall remained side by side at the whiteboard. "Two worlds come together as one," Amy said. "The Mayan civilization and modern time. The effects of the earth in the Dark Rift are not predictable, but they are happening right now. God, why didn't I see this before? I'll bet Mr. Froth figured it out." She decided not to be like Marshall and add a "tricky, tricky."

"Alignment happens on a large scale and a small scale," Marshall added. "Amy showed you the large scale in the center of the Milky Way. The small scale is happening in the center of our school; specifically, the auditorium. All four rooms must have something in common to create this phenomenon. If we locate it, we'll be able to figure this out."

"And just what do they have in common?" Ziggy asked. "Besides walls."

"Projectors," Amanda said. She stood quickly and joined the other two near the whiteboard. "All of the rooms have a projector tied into the network. That's how the Mayans got here, and that's how Mr. Froth got there. Is that what you're thinking, Amy?"

"Yes!" The two girls exchanged a quick hug. Marshall gave out fist bumps.

"I think I get it now," Ziggy said, although Amy still sensed some confusion on his part. Maybe he just wanted to join in the festivities?

"We need to go to the school's dark rift," Amy said.

"To the belly of the beast," Amanda said.

"To the circumcenter," Marshall added.

"To the auditorium!" Ziggy said.

The foursome headed out the door, took a hard right and moved quickly down the hall. Another of those booming sounds filled the hallway as they hurried along. *The Mayan god of earthquakes was working overtime,* Amy thought. Marshall arrived at the auditorium first and yanked hard on the large door handles, only to come up empty. He rubbed his hands together and tried again. The doors wouldn't budge.

"Must be locked from the inside," Marshall said.

The doors had a small opening under them, and Amy saw some odd lights flashing at her feet. This was followed by other strange sounds like creaking and clanging.

"What's going on in there?" Amanda asked.

"I'm not sure," Ziggy said. "There are no windows."

"The side door has one," Amy said. "Let's check it out."

Amy sprinted down the short hallway, and the others followed. She turned the corner and arrived at the side door before the others. It had a small, round window. She tried the handle, but it was locked. Another flash of light nearly blinded her as she pressed her face to the window to see toward the stage. Then she saw them.

"Oh no!"

"What is it, Amy?" Amanda asked.

She turned and gently pushed the others away. She couldn't breathe and started to make gagging noises.

"What's in there?" Marshall asked as he pushed by her. She put her arm out to stop him.

"Mayans," she said. "They're everywhere."

Chapter 11
Ziggy

Ziggy made his way past Amy and looked through the small window. *This is bad,* he thought. The Mayans were dressed in their distinctive multi-colored costumes, and they were all over the place. Some were on the stage, checking out the old curtains and running from the stage to the main floor. Others were taking books off the shelves and examining them. They sure were a curious bunch. Unfortunately, most of the books ended up on the floor. *Wow,* he thought, *if our librarian, Mrs. Hempel, ever caught them, they'd be toast.*

"So what do we do now?" Marshall asked. "This was totally unexpected."

"It's one of those good news, bad news deals," Amanda said. "The good news is they appear to be confined to the auditorium. The bad news is that's where we need to be."

Ziggy knew they needed a new plan, and they needed it quickly. He thought about what had taken place over the course of the day and where they should go next. They couldn't watch the Mayans through the window all day. Mr. Froth said the Mayans were inquisitive by nature, so he and his science fair friends had to stay a step ahead.

"Back to Mr. Froth's room," Amy said. "It should be safe there."

"Wait," Ziggy said. "Wouldn't it be better if we went to Frank's room? It seemed like more of a control center."

"Ziggy's right," Amanda said. "Plan A didn't work, so we go with Plan B."

"But what if *they* are in there too?" Marshall asked, pointing to the Mayans in the auditorium.

"My theory is that they're not," Amanda said. "They returned through the circumcenter."

"We're wasting time arguing," Amy said. "Let's just go."

There was a face staring back at them in the small window in the door, and Ziggy jumped back with a yell. That seemed like a pretty good incentive, so they got out of there as quickly as they could. Two right turns and one left later they were heading down the hall to what they called "Frank's Room." It was a solid door, so Ziggy couldn't tell if the room was being overrun with centuries-old Mayans or if it was just another room in the school. He was daring enough to put his ear up to the door.

"Sounds empty," Ziggy whispered to the others. He grabbed the handle and took a deep breath, hoping with all his heart they weren't the world's quietest Mayans ready to pounce. He exhaled and pulled. The door swung open without a problem, and he peeked in to find a room completely void of Mayan types. Whew! "All clear," he said.

They went around the furnace toward the makeshift classroom and peered in. It looked the same as last time with the projector running, bathing the room in white light. Ziggy joined the others in a collective sigh of relief, knowing they were safe for the time being. Or so it seemed.

"So what's the plan?" Marshall asked. He was looking at Ziggy with his head slightly tilted. "You know. Plan B?"

"I'm not sure," Ziggy said. "We just had to get away from the auditorium, and it seemed like a better idea than Mr. Froth's room."

"You're not sure? You're not sure?" The second one was much louder than the first. "I can't believe this."

Typical midlister, thought Ziggy. So predictable. "Wait a minute," he said as he made the timeout signal. "You guys had the bright idea of going to the auditorium. Five minutes ago, everyone was all 'circumcenter' this and 'belly of the beast' that. What would you have done if the Mayans weren't there?"

"Just admit you don't have a plan, Ziggy."

"As soon as you admit your circumcenter plan was complete bull!"

Marshall took a giant step in Ziggy's direction. "Let's see you Ziggy your way out of this one."

"Hey Marshall, how about you bite me!" Ziggy took a step toward him and felt his right hand form a fist. He was a bit shorter than Marshall but had quickness and agility on his side.

Amanda stepped in front of Ziggy and grabbed his hand. She was stronger than she looked. "Stop it, you two."

"Yeah," Amy said. "This is no time to be macho."

Their 'macho' glaring contest lasted all of five seconds. Not because either one got the upper hand, but because Marshall stepped on the foot of a table and nearly fell over. Ziggy tried his hardest not to laugh as Amy helped Marshall up.

"Now that we're here," Amanda said, "we need to refocus on the task at hand. The Mayans are in the building, and we need to stop them. We're supposed to be the best science minds in the school, so let's figure this out. Ziggy made a good point. What would we have done if we had had access to the auditorium? Can we do it from here?"

"The alignment," Amy said. "That's the cause of everything. Each of the rooms must have something in common."

"Projectors," Ziggy said. "Amanda already said it."

"They're just machines," Marshall added. "Maybe we should just pull the plug."

"No!" Amy said. "Not until we send the Mayans packing."

"And get Mr. Froth and Frank back," Amanda said.

"It's more than just the projectors," Ziggy said. "We've established that they're all networked together. The others go through the school network, and this one is hard-wired through this yellow cable." He held it up to make his point. "That's the only way to communicate."

"Maybe not," Amanda said. She was near the table with the laptop. "Look, one extra wire plugged into the computer. The black one with the white stripe is the power cord, the yellow is the network connector and then there's this one." She held up a thin black wire. It ran down the back, then took a right turn toward the opposite corner. It was covered by one of those extension cord covers so nobody tripped over it, which made it difficult to see against the dark floor. "It's hard-wired to the laptop."

"It comes out here," Marshall said. He followed it up the wall with his finger until it disappeared into the pipes.

"Now what do we do?" Amy asked.

"We have to find out where it goes," Ziggy said. "If it's important enough to be hooked up, it's important enough to follow."

"I found it," Amanda said. "It goes behind that pipe and comes out over there." She pointed to the corner of the room. They all moved to that corner.

"Straight up," Ziggy said. "Then out that vent." There was a small vent high up on the wall. "I'll bet it leads to the roof."

"Is that your hypothesis?" Amy asked.

"Yes," Ziggy said. "I'm thinking it's an antenna or a receiver wire. And what better location for either of them than the roof?"

"There's an outside exit near the back stairwell," Marshall said. "Time to check out the mystery wire. Who's with me?"

"I'll go," Ziggy said. "We can take the fire escape to the roof."

"Well, I'm not staying here," Amy said. "Not with those…those…*people* in the building."

"How about we all go," Amanda said. "You guys can handle the roof climbing. Okay?"

Marshall led the way out the double doors and into the face of a chilly breeze. That end of the building was always windy. Ziggy looked up and located the black wire from the vent, and it indeed went up to the edge of the roof and disappeared over the edge.

"The fire escape," Ziggy said, pointing to the ladder that ran down the back of the building. "We head up this one to the first roof. I'll bet the wire goes all the way to the auditorium roof, though." There was another ladder that went from the shorter roof up the side of the auditorium. "No problem. Right, Marshall?"

They stood beneath the first fire escape ladder and looked up. The first rung was about eight feet off the ground. That kept curious students from going up it on a whim. Ziggy knew that under normal circumstances, anyone caught going up that ladder was automatically suspended; but these circumstances were far from normal.

"You first, Marshall," Ziggy said. "Jump on up there."

He gave it a weak attempt and barely left the ground. Ziggy guessed his oversized feet acted like anchors at times like these. "I can't, Ziggy. It's too high. Just go without me." He started to walk away. "Maybe you should take one of the girls instead."

"Marshall!" Ziggy looked around for something to help him up a bit—a barrel, perhaps—but saw nothing. Finally he locked his fingers together and held them out. "Come on, step here."

Ziggy braced himself for the full effect of Marshall's gigantic foot in his hands. Marshall steadied himself on Ziggy's shoulder and stepped in. Ziggy wobbled a bit as Marshall reached up and grabbed the first rung. With a groan Ziggy lifted him as high as he could. Two rungs. Three rungs. Finally Marshall's right foot found the lowest rung and he was off.

"I'll call you when we get up there," Ziggy said to Amanda and Amy. Two deep breaths later, he was ready to go. He jumped as high as he could and caught the lowest rung with both hands. He raised himself up one rung at a time, convinced he was not going to look like a dork in front of the girls. The brick wall came in handy as his sneakers crept along. Marshall reached the lower roof, and Ziggy was right behind him. Ziggy looked over the ladder and gave the girls a two-finger salute. All was well.

They picked up the trail of the black wire and followed it to the side of the auditorium, where it ran up next to the ladder. This climb required no leaping, thankfully, and they scaled it easily. Ziggy took the opportunity to look around as Marshall came up behind him. The view of the entire school grounds was spectacular from the highest spot on campus.

"No time for sightseeing," Marshall said as he smacked him on the shoulder. "Let's get this over with."

There was a large air-conditioning unit directly ahead of them, its metallic finish glistening in the sunlight. The black wire went around it to the right. They followed it and when they got around to the other side, Marshall stopped so quickly Ziggy nearly walked into him.

"What is that?" Ziggy asked.

The black wire was attached to a small black box about a foot square. On top of that was a six-foot antenna mounted to a tripod.

"It's some sort of receiver, I'd say." Marshall reached over and lifted the black box. It came up easily. "Definitely homemade."

"Maybe it's a transponder," Ziggy said. He had heard that word used on a TV show, and it sounded technical. Marshall did not disagree.

"And check this out," Marshall said as he took a few steps back. "It's in the dead center of the auditorium. Pretty freaky, Zig."

He didn't like to be called Zig but let it go. Marshall did have a point.

"Yeah, freaky. I should call the girls and tell them what we found." Ziggy took out his phone and called Amanda. She picked up on the second ring.

"It took you long enough, Ziggy! What's going on up there?"

Typical girl response, he thought. "We're fine, Amanda. And there's definitely some kind of device up here. Marshall thinks it's a receiver or transponder of some kind. It's attached to an antenna on a tripod. We—"

Before he could finish, the black box began to vibrate and hum. Pretty soon the entire roof began to shake. Marshall grabbed Ziggy's shoulder and began to pull. "Time to go, Ziggy."

They ran to the other side of the air-conditioning unit and peeked back at the apparatus. A bright, yellow spark worked its way in a spiral pattern down the antenna and into the black box. This was followed by a loud *boom!* in the auditorium below them. Ziggy could feel the vibrations through the sheet metal.

"We need to get off this roof," Marshall said. He was two steps ahead of Ziggy as he made a beeline for the ladder. Ziggy took the opportunity to call Amanda back, but she never picked up. How odd.

Marshall went down the ladder much quicker than he went up it. He was on the lower roof in no time. They reached the last ladder simultaneously, but Ziggy squeezed ahead of him and went first. Ziggy hung from the last rung and dropped softly to the ground, then waited for Marshall and helped him as he fell.

"Amanda? Amy?" Ziggy yelled. He figured they must have hidden somewhere when the load noises arrived. He tried to call Amanda again. No answer. He tried Amy. No answer.

"Where are they?" Marshall asked.

"They must have gone back in," Ziggy said. He hoped it was true, but something didn't feel right. Going on the roof seemed like a good idea at the time, but now he regretted leaving them alone.

They sprinted to the back door, and Ziggy flung it open. Marshall flew by him, running as fast as Ziggy had ever seen him go. He arrived at Frank's room and yanked the door open.

"Amy," he yelled. "You in here? Amanda?"

No one answered as they came to the "situation room" in

the back. This time it was Ziggy who stopped too fast, causing Marshall to slam into his back. He didn't feel it. All he could do was point weakly at the screen and say, "Oh no!"

Mr. Froth and Frank were still surrounded by Mayans on top of the pyramid. Amanda and Amy had joined them.

Chapter 12
Ziggy

Both Amanda and Amy were looking right at them, seemingly pleading for help. One Mayan held out Amanda's phone and started poking around with a perplexed look. Marshall's arm was still on Ziggy's shoulder, and he made no effort to move it. Neither of them said a word for several seconds. Then the screen went blank. Marshall's arm slid off, and he quickly found a chair.

"We shouldn't have left them alone," Marshall said. He ran his hands through his thick hair and pulled it back. "What the heck were we thinking, Ziggy? Now those Mayans have all four of them. Plus they have Mr. Froth's iPad and all the smart phones. This is bad. Really bad. I'm talking epic bad." He hung his head in his hands, which, by the way, were proportionally as large as his feet.

Ziggy was losing Marshall at a time when he most needed him. It was time for some serious Ziggy magic. "We could not have seen this coming, Marshall. Splitting up was a team decision and a good one at the time. Now the team is down to two, and we have to work even smarter to find them." He gave Marshall a quick pat on the arm. "You and I can do this. I know we can."

Marshall peeked up at Ziggy with one uncovered eye. "That's it? That's your pep talk?"

"Sorry, it's just that—"

"Hey, I'm just bustin' ya, Zig." This time he smacked Ziggy's arm. "I know what you mean. Plan C to the rescue. You do have a Plan C, right?"

Of course he did. Absolutely. No problem. Just as soon as he could think of it. But before he could, the portable projector screen snapped up like a window blind; and they, in turn, snapped to attention. The images of Amanda and Amy stopped, and they were once again in the soft glow of the white light.

"Was that an accident?" Marshall asked.

"I think so. These old screens have a mind of their own sometimes." Ziggy thought it was best to put the screen back down, so he grabbed the cord and began to pull. He stopped when something on the wall behind it caught his eye. It was hard to see in the projector light, so he blocked the light with his body. Something was written on the cinder blocks.

"What is it, Ziggy?"

He moved closer and made out the words:

Na kab
k'aana

"Great," Marshall said. "I am really getting tired of these Mayan words. What do they mean?"

Ziggy studied the words for a few seconds. *Was it written here recently?* He took his finger and smudged the edge of the "k." It came off easily like it was just put here in magic marker. He had seen the words before on one of Mr. Froth's Mayan vocabulary tests. He closed his eyes and focused as hard as he could on the two words. He wished Amanda was around because she memorized everything easily. He tried to recall what Amanda had showed them about remembering things. Was it in the sensory store, the short-term store or the long-term store? Too many stores! He went back to the old tried-and-true method and said the words out loud several times. And just like that it came to him.

"Thumb and up. It means thumb-up."

"What?" Marshall said. "That makes absolutely no sense unless you're a hitchhiker."

"Ah, but it does. To me it makes perfect sense."

"Oh yeah? How about filling me in?"

The answer came to him like a cold splash of water. Of

course! 'Tricky, tricky Mr. Froth,' to steal Marshall's phrase. "*Chumuk*. That was your keyword, Marshall. *Yaanal* was Amanda's. The whiteboard spelled out *Xibalba be* for Amy. And finally I get *Na kab* and *k'aana*."

"I know all that, Ziggy. I was there, remember?"

"Let me finish." Ziggy loved it when he was on a roll. "Thumbs-up is a visual reference. It helps explain the right hand rule."

"The right hand rule?"

"Yup. That's my contribution to this whole test. Practical application of the right hand rule." He found a pencil and wrapped his fingers around it with his thumb-up to illustrate. "The thumb of my right hand points in the direction of the current flow, and the fingers point in the direction of the magnetic field." He held it straight out for Marshall to see. He seemed less than impressed.

"So what's your plan? Need I remind you we have four people missing and a school full of very curious Mayans?"

Gee thanks, Marshall! I hadn't thought of it in so long, Ziggy thought.

He took the pencil and put it behind his ear in case he needed it later. "My theory is that a magnetic field of very large magnitude is somewhere in the school. We need to find this magnetic field and reverse it."

Marshall gave him a blank look. "That's it? Gee, I hope our old friend, Kisin, the Mayan stinking god of death, doesn't mind. He and his merry band of Mayan citizens look so friendly and accommodating."

Once again, Ziggy could have done without the sarcasm. It was a typical midlister reaction, so he let it slide. "We'll have to deal with them later. First we need to find that magnetic field. Where do *you* think it is, Marshall?"

Marshall put his hands behind his head as he paced. "I don't know what to think anymore, Ziggy. There seems to be something terrible around every corner. If you're asking about

77

my hypothesis, I'd say the answer to everything is in the auditorium. Every clue we've been given has begun or led us there. Think about it, Zig. The memory store, the alignment and the circumcenter. That's three out of three. You really think yours is different? I don't."

This was the most enlightened Ziggy had ever heard Marshall speak. Maybe he was tired. Maybe he was angry. Regardless it was a brilliant analysis of the situation.

"I agree, Marshall. Now we just have to come up with a plan to get back into the auditorium."

"I've been thinking about that too. First things first." He took a chair and leaned it against the handle of the only door into the room. He jiggled it to make sure it was steady. "I feel safer already. Don't want any curious friends coming to visit."

Marshall's hypothesis sparked something in Ziggy. He took the pencil from behind his ear and found a small piece of notebook paper near the laptop. His initial sketch of the auditorium layout was crude; but he liked what he saw, so he slid it over to Marshall.

"Impressive," Marshall said. "But I don't see a lot of room to hide a large magnetic device. The stage was empty; the shelves only had books on them. The only things left are the chairs and the projector cart. Nothing under the chairs, that's for sure."

"The projector cart," Ziggy said. "It had a lower level, remember?"

Marshall shook his head. "Not really. To tell the truth, I wasn't paying much attention to it. Besides it was pretty dark. Plus that stupid countdown voice kept going on and on and—"

"We should try using the associative memory techniques Amanda showed us. Picture yourself back in the chair and recall what you saw." Ziggy closed his eyes for effect. "There's the stage directly in front of us and the screen at the back of it. The projector's on a cart. What color is the cart?"

"I...I don't know. I didn't..." Ziggy took a peek and saw

that Marshall had his eyes closed too. "Wait a Frederick Froth minute," Marshall said. "I see it. It's kind of a silver color, right? And the projector is also silver."

The image popped in Ziggy's head as soon as Marshall said it. "Yes. And the cart is about three feet high with a lower level just above the wheels. Is the lower level empty, Marshall?"

Ziggy could hear him breathe as he pondered that last one.

"No, Ziggy. Something is definitely there. It's a box. Really dark. It reminds me of the one on the roof, only a lot bigger."

"That's it, Marshall! That's the magnetic source. I mean, what else can it be?" Ziggy banged his hand several times on the top of a chair. "Amanda's key word was *Yaanal,* meaning 'under.' Not just under the seats but also under the projector cart. It makes perfect sense."

"Tricky, tricky Mr. Froth," Marshall said, barely beating Ziggy to it.

"Now we just have to get to it."

They both had their eyes open when the room rattled again. The image of their four captured friends flashed on the brick wall. Their heads hung low like they had given up.

"Ziggy, I don't like the odds. The Mayans are everywhere. It seems like they're drawn to every little noise, and they figure things out so quickly. Maybe they're just smarter than us." He hung his head like the others.

"No!" Ziggy yelled. "Don't you give up on me. Come on, Marshall." He shook his friend's shoulders hard. "We don't have much time. We need to network our talents and come up with a plan."

Marshall's large head snapped up quickly. "That's it! The network. I can't believe I didn't think of it earlier." He moved faster than Ziggy had ever seen him. In four massive steps he was at the desk and typing on the laptop. "Mr. Froth could see the entire school from here, Ziggy." *Click. Click. Click.* "And so can we." Ziggy watched as he opened file after file on the desktop. Marshall swore almost under his breath as he closed them.

"What are you looking for, Marshall?"

"Redundancies, Ziggy." His fingers were working at a lightning pace. "Every good system has built-in redundancies. I'm hypothesizing that Mr. Froth put the same apps and the same data on each machine. That's totally what a scientist would do. If any part of the network fails, another machine can be used." He clapped his hands together, and Ziggy jumped a little. "There it is: TimeScope."

He opened a folder and found the program. Ziggy watched over his shoulder as Marshall clicked to open it. Immediately their faces popped up on the display. As Ziggy moved, so did the image on the screen. It was a live camera shot.

He clicked the mouse, and they disappeared from the screen. "I didn't expect that. TimeScope has a built-in webcam."

"So you can record us on the webcam and play it back over the network?" Ziggy asked.

Marshall scanned the options on the screen. "Looks that way, Ziggy. Are you thinking what I'm thinking?"

"Yup. It's time to give our Mayan friends a little taste of modern science."

Chapter 13
Marshall

Neither of them was into drama, but they did the best acting they could. With the computer webcam rolling, Marshall and Ziggy alternated calling out to Mr. Froth and the others as they stood in front of the cinderblock wall.

"Amanda? Where are you? Come on, talk to me." Ziggy said in his most thespian voice. "Amy? Say something!"

"Mr. Froth! Come out, come out, wherever you are!" Marshall added.

"Can you hear me, Frank?" Ziggy pleaded.

They added another minute of heartfelt pleas before stopping. There was no time to edit the production, so Marshall saved it as it was. It wasn't Hollywood, but it was certainly good enough. Yeah, like the Mayans would notice.

"We can send this anywhere in the school, Ziggy. We need to get them in one place." The light from the computer screen shone back in Marshall's face, revealing a silly smile.

"I know," Ziggy said. "I have it narrowed down to the gym or Mr. Froth's room."

Marshall clicked on the school map and brought up the gym. "Too many doors to cover in the gym. Let's try Mr. Froth's room." With another click the blueprint of the room appeared. "Much better. Only two doors going into the hallway. We should be able to secure them."

"I am all over that," Ziggy said.

Next Ziggy gathered some supplies they'd need for the task at hand. He searched the small room in the back and found two brooms with fiberglass handles. He managed to snag some wire and a roll of duct tape hanging on the wall in the corner

"Perfect," Marshall said. "That should buy us enough time."

With a few clicks Marshall sent the recorded image over the network to the projector in Mr. Froth's room. The volume control was limited, and they hoped it was enough.

"Let's see if they take the bait," Marshall said. He was able to access the security cameras in the hallways, and they watched as the Mayans began moving in.

"It's working," Ziggy said. "These Mayans are the most curious folks I've ever seen."

"We don't have much time," Marshall said. "We'll take the north hallway and cut across behind the auditorium."

"Sounds like a plan."

Ziggy gathered the broom handles, wire and duct tape while Marshall moved the chair away from the door. He peeked out into the hallway, then checked around the first corner.

"All clear."

Their plan was to run as fast as they could, then hide in doorways to make sure no Mayans were hanging around the halls. They came to the north hallway, and this time Ziggy looked around the corner. Still clear. They sprinted past the math classrooms and ducked behind one of the English teacher's entry. Ziggy peeked and saw a Mayan heading the other way. They waited ten seconds, then booked it for the middle hallway. Marshall was right behind him the whole time. The big guy was faster than Ziggy expected. They stopped at the last corner before Mr. Froth's room.

"Anyone coming?" Marshall whispered.

A quick check revealed that one door to Mr. Froth's room was open. Three Mayans entered; then the hallway was vacant. "All clear," Ziggy whispered back. "But let's give it a few seconds."

Ziggy could hear Marshall counting under his breath. On the count of five, Ziggy nodded his head; and they made a beeline to Mr. Froth's room. The door closest to them was closed, so Ziggy sneaked a look through the small window and saw the Mayans carefully studying the projected image they had recorded earlier. *I hope we're convincing*, he thought. Ziggy handed Marshall a broom handle, some wire and a roll of duct tape. He secured the closed door by wiring the handle to the doorknob and wrapping tape around the handle. If done properly, the door could no longer be opened outward. Ziggy moved to the open one and gently nudged it closed. He quickly stuck the handle across the frame, then wired and taped it to the door knob. Then Ziggy dropped the tape and ran like mad.

As they escaped up the hall, Ziggy could hear some banging on the door; but he knew they had bought some time. Two right turns later they were at the auditorium.

"That was fun," Marshall said. "They sounded pretty pissed off."

"We're not in the clear yet." Ziggy looked in the window once, twice, three times before he was convinced the auditorium was free of Mayans. "Let's go." He swung open the door just enough for them to squeeze through, thankful that the Mayans had unlocked it. Not much had changed since the last time they were there except the chairs were knocked over.

"This is it," Marshall said as he examined the projector cart. "You were right, Ziggy." There was a large metal box on the lower rack. Closer inspection revealed two cables running from the box. One went to the projector on the upper rack, and the other took off toward the corner.

"I'll bet this connects with the unit on the roof," Ziggy said. "Now we need to figure out how to reverse the field."

"What do you mean 'figure out?' I thought this was, you know, your specialty. You better know how to do this, Ziggy."

There were two latches on each side of the box. Ziggy unsnapped all of them like he knew what he was doing. "The right hand rule shows you a visual of the magnetic flow. I just have to reverse it." There was just enough room to remove the lid of the box. He lifted it and pulled it away. "Okay, this looks familiar. We have a magnetic coil. I used two of them in my experiment." He pointed to a small device next to the coil.

"This is an ammeter, which measures amperage. And that's the power supply. Pretty basic set-up."

"We don't have much time," Marshall said. His right foot thumped loudly next to the cart.

"I know. It's just a matter of reversing the flow. You know, making the thumb-up into a thumb-down." There were two extra wires he couldn't explain. They ran out of the power supply, across the floor and back up into the corner, along with the network cable—to the roof, he figured.

"Tickety, tick, tick." Marshall tapped his watchless wrist.

"I know, and that's not helping." Ziggy unscrewed the two wires leading from the power supply to the coil and reversed them. That had to be it. "Okay, the field is reversed. What went down will now go up. And vice versa." Ziggy was so confident he had it right, he began to put the lid back on. He gave Marshall a nod as he snapped it shut. "Now let's get out of here."

Marshall led the way, first checking for Mayans in the hallway as they dashed back to the control room. Ziggy closed the door and secured it with a chair. So far it appeared the Mayans had not found out about their room.

"Time to switch rooms," Marshall said as he worked at the computer. With a click he made their searching-for-the-others video play in the auditorium.

"Do you think the Mayans are out yet?" Ziggy asked.

"Let's find out."

He switched to the hallway monitors and found one that showed Mr. Froth's room from down the hall. The door closest to the camera pushed out against the broom handle several times. Finally a surge of Mayans broke through and spilled out into the hallway. Marshall figured even among the mighty Mayans, sometimes brute force was the only way.

"Do you think they'll notice that it's the same video?" Ziggy asked.

"Not likely. The whole idea is centuries ahead of them. In

fact, I'm going to crank it up just to make sure they know we're in the auditorium." He slid a control on the screen all the way to the right. Ziggy just had to trust that it was as loud as it could go.

The Mayans seemed to be listening carefully as they made their way down the hallway toward their pleading voices. A camera near the auditorium showed them entering through the double doors. A fat one brought up the rear and seemed to be puffing as he entered.

"Now for TimeScope to do its thing," Marshall said. "I'll just bring it up." He stared at the main menu for five seconds, then ten, then fifteen.

"I'm thinking now would be a really good time, Marshall."

He studied the screen some more. Ziggy couldn't tell if Marshall, with his constant foot tapping, was scared or in really deep thought. Either way, it was taking way too long.

"Marshall, do something! I thought you knew how to do this."

"Shut up, Ziggy. I'm trying to think. It was a pull-down menu from the main page in the other room." He tapped the keyboard nearly as quickly as his feet. "Here it is!" He hit "return" with a resounding snap.

The boom was the loudest one of the day. The screen of the laptop nearly tipped forward from the jolt.

"Are they gone?" Ziggy asked.

"I don't know. Let's see if there's a camera in the auditorium." Ziggy turned his attention to the screen while Marshall accessed the video system. "I think this is it." It was grainier than the other camera shots, but they could make out the main part of the auditorium. It appeared to be empty.

"Where are the girls and Mr. Froth?" Ziggy asked. "And Frank, of course."

"I'm not sure." He looked at the projector screen, then back at the laptop screen. "Unless..." The mouse began to move around the screen.

"Unless what?"

"Of course! Why didn't I see it before?"

"See what? Come on, Marshall. Where are they?"

He grinned as he typed away. "Built-in redundancies, Ziggy. It's one of the principles of TimeScope. When one system fails—"

"Another is there to take its place. Like the system in Mr. Froth's classroom. Or the one in his lab."

"It works both ways, Ziggy. The redundant systems can work separately or together. In this case, Mr. Froth placed the systems in the outer rooms. We need all three doing the same thing at the same time. The Mayans figured it out, and that's how they got here. And that, my friend, is how we'll get the others back."

"The circumcenter, right, Marshall?"

He looked up me. "Now you're catching on, Zig. I'm going to set up TimeScope in the other two rooms."

"What do I do?"

"Stay here and wait for my call. When I give the word, click on the 'start' button on this page. Got it?"

Ziggy gave him a two-finger salute, and Marshall took off out the door. Ziggy watched him on the school video camera as he ran down the halls. He disappeared into the science lab first. After a minute, he took a left turn and headed down the hall to Mr. Froth's room. Ziggy's cell phone was ready and waiting. The call came two minutes later, and Ziggy put it on "speaker."

"All set, Ziggy. Hit the 'start' button."

Ziggy clicked the large triangle. "Done."

The boom wasn't as loud as the previous one, but Ziggy sure felt it. "I think it worked," he said to Marshall.

There was a clicking sound, followed by faint voices coming from Marshall's phone. "Marshall? Talk to me, man. What's happening down there?" Ziggy checked the video of the auditorium, and no one had appeared. He switched to the hallway cameras, and the school appeared to be empty. He could still hear faint sounds from his phone.

"Uh oh!" Marshall's voice crackled then faded. "Zig—"
Then the video feed turned to snow. Ziggy switched to the other cameras, but there was no feed. "Marshall? Marshall?"
His phone went silent.

Chapter 14
Ziggy

Ziggy punched in Marshall's number, but it never rang. How strange… He had no way of knowing what was happening in other parts of the school. The video feed went from snow to a blank screen. It appeared the entire network was down.

Okay, it was time for action. *But what type of action?* He had to get out of this room, the only safe room in the school, and see what was going on with his own eyes. Ziggy's brain knew what to do, but his feet could not be convinced. He stood, frozen, staring at the white light on the screen. He had no concept of time even though he could see the clock on the computer screen. *Was this part of the test? What was the point of the test anyway?* Too many crazy thoughts were turning his brain to mush.

He heard a voice. It wasn't a real voice his ears could pick up but rather one of those voices inside his head. Was it Amy? No, it sounded more like Amanda. Maybe it didn't matter.

"Move it, Ziggy," the voice said.

His feet finally cooperated. They walked him out the door and down the long hallway. His plan was to figure out what happened to Marshall.

The first stop was the auditorium. He peeked in through the window in the double doors. Empty. It looked like reversing the magnetic field and the right hand rule had worked for getting rid of the Mayans.

The next stop was Mr. Froth's room. The closest door was a mess with the broom handle snapped in pieces on the floor of the hallway. He looked in with a series of quick head jerks in case "someone" was still in there. It appeared to be empty too.

He was about to leave when the projector screen began to roll up. Written on the board behind it was something he had seen before:

$$\Phi_B$$

It was crudely drawn, but he got the basic idea. It was the symbol for magnetic flux. *What did flux have to do with anything?* All the previous clues were in Mayan, but Ziggy was pretty sure there was no way to represent that word in Mayan. Flux. Flux. Flux. *So what?*

Then he thought back to his science project. He had used flux to help explain the right hand rule and its relationship to magnetic fields. He found a cool definition somewhere on the internet and modified it for the project. He scrunched his eyes to come up with it. Then it popped in his head:

Flux - The amount of stuff that goes through your area

He was proud of himself for coming up with the definition, but what did it really mean? Okay, back to the science project. The problem was that reversing the field allowed the Mayans to go back but did not allow the others to come this way. It was the perfect use of the right hand rule—in reverse—but still it did not completely work.

His hypothesis was still a work in progress. He must have missed something in his earlier solution. The box under the projector in the auditorium had a single magnetic coil, an ammeter and a power source. Something was missing. He snapped his fingers as it came to him. The second magnetic coil, of course.

So what's the connection between flux and a second magnetic coil?

He smacked himself on the side of the head to help with the hypothesis. *I am a downlister, so this sort of thinking is supposed to be second nature to me. Think. Think. Think.*

For the first time in a long time the head smack worked. The light bulb went on: it really was all about flux. He realized the combined size of the two magnetic coils put out more flux than just the one he reversed. He needed to reverse the other one. Hypothesis complete.

Solution: he needed to go back up on the roof.

His feet were now in synch with his brain as they sped him out of the classroom and into the empty hallway. He felt his blood pumping as he zoomed past the still-empty auditorium toward the side entrance. He turned the corner near the back stairs and stopped dead in his tracks.

He was standing nearly face to face with Kisin, the Mayan god of death.

Kisin stood there with his right hand clutching a spear at his side while making a snarling sound. His dark features and long hair looked even more menacing in the poor light of the back stairwell. True to his name, the "stinking one" was putting out quite an odor.

Ziggy knew he had to get to the roof, but there was no way he was going through or around the Mayan god of death. He figured he had three things going for him: 1) he was younger, 2) he was probably faster and 3) he knew the layout of the school. It was time to take advantage of all three.

"*Ka'ka'te*," Ziggy said while giving him a two-finger salute. That meant "later" in Mayan. He hoped. It may have meant "sausage." Either way he was out of there.

Ziggy made the first turn at full speed and didn't look back. Based on the layout of the school, he knew it was best to hit the middle hallway and take the stairwell to the second floor from there. He managed to sneak a peek behind as he jetted past the language classrooms. Kisin was coming his way.

He knew he could extend his lead on the stairs. He took them two at a time and turned left toward social sciences. There was a short hallway that branched off this one further down. If he could make it to the elevator, ol' Kisin would have no idea where he went. His heart raced as he made the right turn and pushed the button for the elevator. The school put it in a few years ago to comply with some handicapped regulations. Unfortunately the car was on the lower floor, and he had to wait for it. Mr. Kelley's science classroom was close by so he pressed his back against the door and tried to breathe. The elevator door opened, and he quickly entered and pushed the button for the ground floor. He was in the clear.

He never saw the spear. It struck the back of the elevator and bounced off the wall. Kisin came toward him just as the door closed, and Kisin pounded on it as the elevator began to move. The ride to the ground floor took forever, or so it seemed. When the door opened, Ziggy stuck his head out just enough to look up and down the hallway. Fortunately for him, the school wasn't configured with a stairwell right next to the elevator.

He chose to go right and avoid the major hallway. The back way past the Industrial Ed room seemed like the best return route. It was a section of the school he rarely saw because most honor students never really got the chance to take Industrial Education. A left turn put him on the path to the back exit and the way up to the roof. He peeked first and it was clear. Part of him wondered where Kisin was, and another part hoped he'd never find out.

He opened the back door as quietly as he could, slowly pushing the long handle with both hands. The cool blast of air startled him for a second, but he recovered to guide the door closed. There was still no sign of El Stinko, and Ziggy gave a short fist pump as he made his way to the fire escape ladder.

Maybe he was tired, but the ladder seemed much higher off the ground than last time. With a deep breath he jumped as high as he could and caught the lowest rung with both hands, then slipped off. Another voice in his head, possibly Amy's, encouraged him along. He tried again after wiping his hands on his pants, but this time he held on and walked up the wall as his hands made their way up the ladder. The roof seemed bigger than last time, probably because he was alone. He quickly found the ladder to the auditorium roof and up he went.

The air-conditioning unit looked bigger too. Sheesh! He began to wonder if he had shrunk since the last visit. *Just focus.* Mr. Froth's contraption was still in the middle of the roof thankfully, and he ran over to it. The plan was to open the box, figure out the design and reverse the magnetic field to balance the flux according to the right hand rule. It sounded easy in his head, but that rarely mattered. His head had let him down many times before. He knelt down and loosened the snaps on the black box under the tripod. It was nearly the same set-up as the one in the auditorium, only a bit smaller. He quickly identified the magnetic coil on one side and some mystery device on the other. It had to be whatever made the people appear and the rooms go *boom.* Regardless he stuck to the task at hand.

The two wires were attached to the magnetic coil using alligator clips, which are small clips with jagged, hinged jaws. It seemed simple enough, so he put red to black and black to red. Moving quickly, he placed the cover back on and got away from it. He wasn't sure exactly how it worked, but it seemed like people came and went when they got too close to it for too long.

Finally he had time to take a huge breath and let it out. The stage was set for the others to return, and all he had to do was go find them in the school. That task was easier than he thought.

Until he saw Kisin coming straight toward him.

How did he find me? Ziggy thought as he backed away. Kisin moved slowly around the air-conditioning unit, then stopped and removed a small knife from his belt. The blade glinted in what was left of the daylight. The only way out was to go around or through the snarling, stinking god of death; but neither seemed very promising. It was time for a new plan.

The only chance he had was to see if the transponder was

working the way he hoped. He felt his pockets and was relieved to find two things: some wire left over from their work on Mr. Froth's door and his phone. He took the phone out and set the stopwatch app for ten seconds. The tone would play a crazy tune when it was finished. He quickly placed it on top of the box. The antenna on the unit was flexible fortunately, so he pulled it over and kept his distance from the box. He tied the wire to the top of the antenna and pulled it even farther, so it was nearly touching the ground. *It might just work!*

Kisin gave him an odd look and laughed a deep laugh. Ziggy must have seemed like easy prey to a warrior like him. He moved the knife from one hand to the other, then back. What a show-off! Ziggy stood on the wire with his arms behind his back, chest out, daring the warrior to come his way. If he could freeze Kisin long enough, the flux was now sufficient to send him back. At least that was the theory. He trusted the right hand rule would not let him down.

"*Taal*!" Ziggy said in his most menacing voice. "*Taal*!" That meant "come."

Kisin laughed and flashed a semi-toothless grin as he began to walk his way. Ziggy had to get Kisin as close to the transponder as possible. Kisin made it easy and walked directly toward it as the phone countdown displayed in large numbers.

"*K'áaba* Ziggy," Ziggy said. "My name is Ziggy."

Kisin flashed the knife at him. "*Ts'o'okol*!" Ziggy was pretty sure that meant "finish."

One more step, big guy. Just one more step.

Kisin had started to walk around the transponder when the alarm went off. He froze and Ziggy took his foot off the antenna wire. The antenna snapped straight up and struck Kisin solidly in the forehead. The knife went flying, and the Mayan god of death stood in stunned silence.

"*Ho'okol*!" Ziggy said. That meant "leave."

And with a spark and a boom, "the stinking one" was gone.

It worked. It worked. It really worked. Ziggy wanted to

stick around and celebrate, but it was time to get off the roof. He hustled past the transponder, around the A/C unit and to the first ladder. He quickly looked to make sure no one else was on the roof. It appeared to be just him. Down that ladder he went, then across the roof to the final ladder. Another look around revealed that he was still alone, so he climbed down and dropped softly to the ground. He wanted to run into the school; but his legs refused, so he just sat against the brick wall and laughed the biggest laugh he could remember.

Chapter 15
Ziggy

It only took a minute or so to reenergize, and Ziggy was curious to know what happened to everyone. He yanked open the back door with a purpose and entered the hallway, hoping there were no more Mayans roaming around. He had reached his limit.

"Ziggy!" he heard someone yell out. It was Amanda (definitely not a Mayan). She ran toward him and gave him the biggest hug he had ever had.

"You're okay, right?" he asked. "Everybody's okay?"

"We're fine and you, sir, were absolutely awesome." She gave him another hug, and he didn't resist.

"How did you know? I thought you were—"

"Let's just say, we saw it all, Ziggy." Her arm was around his waist as they walked down the hall. He didn't know what was going on and didn't really care.

A left turn took them down the main hallway toward the gym. Amy popped out of a door way and stood in front of him.

"You are a superstar of the highest order, Ziggy Zygmont." Her hug came quickly and was slightly awkward, but he adjusted. She smiled like he had never seen her smile. "You kicked some major Mayan butt."

They were now a trio, a real Ziggy cookie, locked arm-in-arm down the main hallway of their school late on a Saturday afternoon. He had this strange feeling they knew much more than he did.

"Zig!" It was the unmistakable sound of Marshall. He joined their group from behind and slapped Ziggy hard on both shoulders. "I knew you'd figure it out. Everyone was worried about that last coil, but I had faith in my Zig. I knew you'd come through."

"Thanks, Marshall. Wait a minute." Ziggy stopped the train, and Marshall nearly ran into him. "Who's everyone?"

They were near the gym now, and Ziggy expected them to turn left toward the auditorium. Instead Amy took one hand and Amanda took the other.

"Everyone," Amanda said, "including the four of us."

"And Frank and Mr. Froth," added Amy.

"And, of course," Marshall said, "the Mayans."

They led him through the swinging doors and into the gym. The place was crawling with Mayans in colorful costumes. *I must have failed*, Ziggy thought. *Why were the Mayans still here?* He tried to back-pedal, but his female friends held him in place.

"Whoa. It's okay, Ziggy," Amanda said. "The test is over."

"Yeah," said Amy. "It's not what you think."

It was an odd thing to say because he didn't know what to think. He just risked his life to save everyone from the Mayans, and now they were all sharing the gym. The confusion overwhelmed him, and there was only one thing left to do.

"Time out. Time out. Time out." Ziggy's hands made the world's most perfect T, and he held it out for all to see. "What are they doing here?" He pointed in the general direction of the Mayans, who, oddly enough, were talking and backslapping like it was some sort of party.

"Zachary Zygmont!" His name rang out from behind. There were two people who called him that on a regular basis: his mom and Mr. Froth. It was clearly not his mom. "That was an impressive practical application of the right hand rule," Mr. Froth said. He didn't look too bad for someone who had been captured by Mayans. He held out his hand and Ziggy shook it. "And flux. Let's not forget flux."

By now, they were wandering through the horde of Mayans in the center of the gym. Only now they didn't look so much like Mayans. They looked, well, like regular twenty-first century folks in funny costumes. Like Halloween.

Ziggy heard someone growl behind him and he turned.

"Taal!" It was Kisin. "Come!" is what he said. He still had a small mark on his forehead where the antenna had whacked him. *Okay, maybe this wasn't so cool after all,* Ziggy thought. He started to back up; then Kisin's growl turned into a laugh. "Well-played, Zachary. Well-played."

He wanted to do another time-out, but his first attempt was roundly ignored. Something weird was going on, and he decided to just go with the flow. Amanda was next to him so he grabbed her hand and held on tightly. "I'm guessing the Mayans aren't really Mayans, right?"

"Not even close," she said as she patted his hand with her free one. "These are the guys who run the science fairs in the area, Ziggy. They're part of the regional test. Pretty amazing, huh?"

"May I have your attention, please?" Mr. Froth said into a wireless microphone. A small amplifier near the stands supplied the sound. "I've taken the liberty of inviting a few guests to this afternoon's festivities. Frank, would you show our guests in?"

Frank ambled over and opened the side door of the gymnasium. Ziggy's parents came in, along with the parents of the other three students. His mom and dad waved to him and took a seat in the front row of the stands. *Okay, I didn't expect that,* Ziggy thought.

"I'd now like to introduce the science fair regional director, Mr. Brayden Cushing."

Mr. Froth handed a second microphone to the guy dressed as Kisin who, in turn, gave Mr. Froth a hardy slap on the shoulder. Then Mr. Cushing removed his headgear and tossed it aside.

"Whew. I hope I won't be needing *that* for a while." He shook his head quickly like he was getting out of the cobwebs. "What we've witnessed today can best be described in one word: incredible. These four students—Amanda, Marshall, Amy and Ziggy—have demonstrated extraordinary knowledge of the main topics defined in their science projects. When we started this interactive testing method two years ago, we had no idea how it would evolve. None. Well, I'm happy to say it has served us well, thanks to teachers like Mr. Froth who came up with the rubric for these students. Simply amazing. How about a hand for the four students and their teacher?" He tucked the mike under his arm and started clapping. Everyone else did too.

Mr. Froth motioned for the students to join him. They arrived as a group, shoulder to shoulder; and he shook hands with each of them. "It wasn't easy coming up with the test concepts for these four unique projects; but thanks to my fellow science teachers, we managed. By the way, you all make an excellent group of Mayans. A special thanks to Mr. Cushing for helping me with the TimeScope software. No, it's not possible to move through time. It is possible to move to the basement, which is where all our time travelers ended up. The project is still in the infant stage, but it worked well enough even for Zachary Zygmont to figure out how to reverse it. Gotta love the right hand rule. Of course, we loved all the projects. GPS accuracy, memory tests, the Dark Rift: these were all well-presented and most importantly, you showed..." He pointed right at them.

"Practical application," the foursome said together.

"Exactly. Now that's my idea of science. As for the future, well, that's up to Mr. Cushing and his team to decide. They'll visit the projects at the other schools and make their decision within the week. I believe any of these could go on to the state competition. Thank you all for coming today and good luck to our four finalists." He turned the mike off and put it back in the stand before joining a small group of Mayans nearby. By now, Ziggy's parents looked like they were itching to see him, so the team shared a final group hug. No words were needed.

Ziggy's mom got to him first. "Zachary, that was just

wonderful." She hugged him, not even caring that it was in front of his friends.

"How long have you guys been here?" he asked.

"Since just after lunch," his dad said. "Mr. Froth called us this morning and invited us to watch from the basement room. Did you know they had cameras all over this school?"

"We got to see everything from down there," his mom said before Ziggy could answer. "We had no idea what was going on until Amanda and Amy showed up. That Amy is so nice, Zach. I hope she's one of your friends too."

Ziggy wanted to tell her they were all his friends. Anyone who could survive an ordeal like this had to be a friend. They posed for pictures, then made their way to the front door. He could tell the day had taken its toll on all of them.

"Goodbye, Ziggy," Amanda said as she gave him one last hug. "You were great today."

"We were all great today. Right, Marshall?" Ziggy held out his fist to bump.

"You got it, Zig." He held out an open hand instead; and Ziggy shook it, then turned it into a bro hug.

Amy stood in Ziggy's path as he turned. She put her hands on his shoulder and whispered something in his ear. "*In laak.*"

"What?" He thought about it for a second, then realized she was speaking Mayan. *Friend.* He couldn't help but notice her smile before she walked away.

"Thanks," he said.

It was cold and dark when Ziggy left the school that evening. He walked out and waited on the top step, enjoying the fresh evening air. He thought about his three cohorts and what Mr. Froth had put them through. They were science fair finalists, not geeks, nerds or dorks, as others had tried to label them over the years. More importantly, they were winners.

He caught a glimpse of his parents and "the beast" in the parking lot and started down the steps. As he put up the hood of his sweatshirt, something made him turn once more. Sure enough, there was Mr. Frederick Froth standing in the large window above the exit with his arms folded. Ziggy wondered how many other students he would be able to reach like he had reached the science fair winners. He noticed the others had stopped and looked too. Mr. Froth raised his hands and snapped his fingers.

And he was gone.

Perfect.

THE END

81454257R00059

Made in the USA
Columbia, SC
01 December 2017